Embrace the
Know where

– Wendy

THE FLANNIGAN GIRLS

a novel

WENDY HALLER

The Flannigan Girls

Produced and printed by Stillwater River Publications.

Visit our website at **www.StillwaterPress.com** for more information.

First Stillwater River Publications Edition

ISBN: 978-1-963296-54-9

Names: Haller, Wendy, author.
Title: The Flannigan girls : a novel / Wendy Haller.
Description: First Stillwater River Publications edition. | West Warwick, RI, USA : Stillwater River Publications, [2024]
Identifiers: ISBN: 978-1-963296-54-9 (paperback)
Subjects: LCSH: Sisters--Fiction. | Psychic trauma in children--Fiction. | Security (Psychology)--Fiction. | Child abuse--Fiction. | Friendship--Fiction. | Families--Fiction. | LCGFT: Domestic fiction.
Classification: LCC: PS3608.A548299 F53 2024 | DDC: 813/.6--dc23

1 2 3 4 5 6 7 8 9 10

Written by Wendy Haller.
Cover and interior design by Elisha Gillette.
Published by Stillwater River Publications, West Warwick, RI, USA.

This book is dedicated to all the amazing women in my life, my sisters, my friends. I am so grateful for you all. Thank you for being by my side on this journey through life.

"In some ways, siblings and especially sisters were more influential in your childhood than your parents."

— Deborah Tannen

ONE

Two-year-old Claire woke up screaming from a night terror. "Mommy! Mommy!" Her sisters jumped out of their beds in the bedroom they shared and rushed over to her. Becca scooped Claire into her arms and hugged her tight while Elana crawled onto the other side of the toddler bed.

"I want mommy," Claire whimpered in her little voice. Becca gave her baby sister a gentle squeeze and laid her back down next to Elana. The ten-year old walked to their bedroom door and out into the hallway. As she slowly walked down the narrow hall, she could hear noises coming from the television in the living room. Her parents were sitting side by side on the couch.

Becca stood behind the couch, she knew once the girls were in bed, they were not to bother their mother unless it was an absolute emergency. "Mom," she said quietly. "Mom, Claire had a bad dream and she's asking for you."

"Oh, Becca," her mother's voice was filled with annoyance, "Dad and I just sat down to watch our show. Get her some milk and put her back to bed. She'll be fine." She shooed her away with the wave of her hand not turning around to make eye contact with her eldest.

Her father looked over his shoulder and nodded his chin toward the kitchen, giving her a small, encouraging smile as if to say, do what your mother asked you to do.

Becca turned and walked toward the kitchen. She took the milk out of the refrigerator and grabbed one of Claire's sippy cups from the drying rack next to the sink. She filled the cup halfway with milk, then put the milk container back into the refrigerator. As she walked back down the hallway, she could hear her parents laughing at whatever was on TV.

Becca walked back into the girls' room and handed the cup to Claire. Elana looked up at her with expecting eyes as if to say, 'Where's Mom?'

Instead of saying anything, Becca picked Claire up and took her over to her own bed. "Come on Claire bear, you can sleep with me tonight."

"And Laney, too?" Claire asked with tears on her cheeks.

"Yes, Laney too."

Seven-year-old Elana grabbed Claire's favorite stuffed bear from her bed. All three girls crawled into Becca's twin size bed. Claire was sandwiched between her two older sisters. Laney handed Claire her bear. They snuggled up together in Becca's bed, finding comfort in each other.

As they curled up to go back to sleep, Elana whispered to Becca over Claire's soft, brown hair, "Flannigan girls stick together."

***

As Claire Rhodes walked down the stairs, her mind flashed to the distant memory. She wasn't sure if it was her own memory or one that had been told to her by her sisters. She didn't think about the years of loneliness without her sisters each day. It came to her out of nowhere. She didn't dwell on all the times she felt neglected by her mother, but she felt it deep in her soul daily.

She shook off the memory as she walked over to her grandfather's old roll top desk. She only had but one wish for herself: to be a loving mother to her own children. She sat down in the antique office chair knowing it was time to get back to her reality.

"Okay, which bills get paid this month?" she asked herself. There was a pile of papers covering her laptop that did not answer. This was her least favorite night of the month. Claire dreaded sitting down and facing the debt roulette, yet here she was, shuffling through bills, and firing up her laptop in their quaint 1950's Cape Cod style home. There was a time when they were able to pay all of their monthly expenses, but not anymore. "Babe, have you seen the spreadsheet for paying bills?"

"I told you I put it in a Google doc titled WE'RE BROKE. Search for it," Claire's husband, Patrick, yelled from across the house.

"Oh, that's right." The mother of three typed the words in the search bar, then yelled, "Was it we're apostrophe e-r or we are? two words?"

"Doesn't matter either way it will show up," he yelled back. She typed the words in the search bar and hit enter.

Oh, there you are. She looked over her shoulder and yelled back across the house to Patrick. "Found it!"

From upstairs her daughter, Gemma, screamed down at her, "Mom, I have a project due tomorrow and I need three pieces of posterboard in different colors."

Why does every conversation I have with my family seem to be screamed from different rooms across the house?

From the kitchen, her son, Grayson, yelled, "We never have anything good to eat in this house." The refrigerator door slammed. He walked into the living room. "By the way, I was supposed to bring in five dollars today with my permission slip signed. My teacher said if it's not in by tomorrow I can't go on the field trip."

"Wait, what field trip? And what do you mean it was due today? I don't remember even seeing a permission slip for a field trip." Claire turned to look at him and saw he had obviously found something to eat as he was munching on some corn chips.

She rolled her eyes at him; they had finished dinner a little over an hour ago. Four-year-old Brita, in tutu and fairy wings, shuffled over and placed a book in her lap, "Read *Goodnight, Angel*?" she asked in her sweet little voice.

Claire shook her head and yelled, "Babe, I need your help!"

"I'm doing something," Patrick yelled back.

"Quit hiding and get in here, please," she said through smiling gritted teeth as she looked down at her youngest child. Claire wanted to get the Sunday night to-do list out of the way so she could start the bedtime routine. She knew many of her mom friends who dreaded the nightly rituals, but Claire loved those extra moments of one-on-one time while tucking the kids into bed. It was something her parents never did for her and her sisters.

"I'll be right there."

Patrick walked into the room and flapped Brita's wings from behind. She looked up at him with adoring eyes as only a daddy's little girl can. This man, who became her partner in life, who filled all the missing holes that had been left in her heart by her own family.

"Did I tell you I bought a lottery ticket for tonight's drawing?" Patrick asked.

Claire shook her head. "How many times do I have to tell you we are not those people. We work for a living. We do not win the lottery."

Patrick walked over and kissed her on the top of her head. He teasingly replied, "Why not? Someone has to win. Why can't it be us?"

After fourteen years of marriage, he still knew how to make her laugh. "Because we are not the one in one million people. Now please focus, I need your help. Gemma has a project due tomorrow, Grayson needs five dollars for a field trip, and his permission slip signed, and Brita needs a bath." She looked down at her little fairy who was sitting on the floor flipping through the pages of her book. Claire directed her attention back to the computer. Patrick picked up Brita.

"Come on, munchkin. Time for a bath." Brita giggled as she hung upside down over her father's shoulder.

"Actually, I don't want to do this right now. Can you help Gemma with her project, and I'll give Brita a bath. I don't have it in me tonight to deal with a meltdown from Gemma."

"Sure. What does she need?" he said as he put Brita back down. She climbed onto Claire's lap.

"Supposedly, three poster boards all in different colors."

Patrick looked at her with a blank stare. "Do we have those?"

"I don't know. You'll have to check the basement. Honestly, I don't even care. She waited until the last minute. She can have all the same color." Patrick headed down to the basement to look for the posterboard. "I hate Sunday nights," Claire said as she minimized the window. "Guess I'll have to not pay a bill later. Come on you. Let's get you cleaned up." She picked Brita up and headed for the stairs.

She got halfway up the stairs when Patrick yelled from the basement, "I can't find any poster board."

She yelled back down to him. "It's at the bottom of the stairs, on the left, on top of the bins labeled school supplies."

"I don't see any!" he yelled. Claire put her daughter down and walked down the basement stairs. Turned to the left and took three pieces of posterboard off of the top of the bin labeled school supplies.

"Here you go." She handed them to him.

"Oh, didn't see it there." Their eyes met and they both half smiled at each other.

"Mmmhmmm..." Claire walked back up the stairs and picked up Brita while shaking her head at how oblivious he could be sometimes. She turned to Brita, "I really don't know, Brita, I really don't know?"

"Know what, Mama?" she asked.

"Anything." Claire carried Brita into the bathroom. She turned on the bath water, put the plug down for the drain and began to help Brita get undressed. "Bubbles or no bubbles?" she asked.

"Bubbles, Mama. Lots and lots of bubbles." Claire took a bottle of Mr. Bubble from the edge of the tub, squeezed a decent amount into the water.

"*Mom!*" A blood curdling scream came from down the hall.

"What now?" she grumbled under her breath. Everything was a crisis for Gemma.

"I need three different colored poster boards. I can't use all white!" Annoyance rolled off Gemma's tongue.

"You should have thought of that before seven o'clock on a Sunday night!" Claire yelled back.

"Why am I always the neglected child in this house," Gemma screamed back at her. Claire rolled her eyes while checking the bath water's temperature. *She has no idea what neglected is.* She picked Brita up and placed her into the mounds of bubbles that had foamed up.

Patrick came to the bathroom door. "I'll run her over to Staples and get the poster board."

Claire sighed heavily. "No, she needs to learn we need more notice. Let her figure it out." Claire stopped for a moment as she heard her own mother's voice coming out of her mouth.

"Are you sure?" he groaned. "Is this a battle you want to have?"

"No, but by the time you run to Staples, buy the poster board and get back, she could already be halfway done with whatever project this is." Claire grabbed a face cloth and began washing Brita.

"Okay. Whatever you think," he relented and walked down the hall. Claire listened as her pissed off daughter told her husband that they were the worst ever and she's going to get points taken off for not following directions and that they don't care about her at all. *The preteen years are the worst.*

"Don't you love as parents how we are blamed for everything," Claire vented to Brita who nodded in agreement while blowing bubbles off her hand. "She forgot about her project, she needs three different colored poster boards and somehow, it's our fault. Gemma is twelve. Twelve! She hasn't even reached her teenage years yet. Is twelve the terrible twos of the teen years?"

Brita laughed. "You're silly, Mama."

I am not prepared for this, Claire thought to herself.

When Claire became a mother, she swore she was going to be the most loving, caring, involved parent ever. She wanted to be everything her mother was not for her. Justine Flannigan never had time for her own daughters. They were another thing on her daily to-do list to take care. Claire hadn't considered the teenage years when making the plan, now she felt like Gemma was acting more like a spoiled brat than an overly loved child. *If these battles are a precursor of what's to come, I may jump in the car and move to Canada for Gemma's teenage years and then return when she goes to college. Maybe I'll take Grayson with me since he's the easiest of the three and fun to travel with. Speaking of...where is he?*

"Patrick?" Claire yelled down the hallway while soaping up Brita's hair.

"Yeah?" he yelled back.

"Where's Grayson?" Brita was hiding herself amongst the bubbles while Claire yelled back and forth with Patrick.

"He ran next door to Kyle's house."

Claire picked up a handful of bubbles and blew them at Brita.

"Can you call him back? He needs to get ready for the school week too?"

Brita was laughing at the bubbles on her nose.

"You got it!"

Grayson was Claire and Patrick's ten-year old son. He got squished in the middle of his sisters. He didn't seem to mind as he was left alone to do all of the things he loved to do, mostly playing video games, and hanging out with his friends.

"Okay, peanut, close your eyes so mama can rinse the shampoo out of your hair." Claire grabbed a cup and filled it with water from the faucet. Brita giggled as Claire poured the water over her head like a waterfall coming down on top of her. They repeated the process until all the shampoo was rinsed out of Brita's hair.

"Do you want to stay in the bath until all of the water drains out?" Claire asked her.

"Yes." Brita blew bubbles off of her hand onto the bathtub wall.

Brita was not a planned pregnancy. Claire and Patrick had given away all their baby stuff after Grayson. They had a girl and a boy, so they didn't feel the need to try for another, it was all even, so they thought they were done. Seven years later, surprise! Claire stood and began to clean the bathroom. She got the towel and baby powder ready for Brita.

"Mom!" Gemma screamed down the hall.

"What?" Claire shouted back.

"Half of my markers are all dried out." Claire could hear exasperation in Gemma's voice.

Whose fault was that? Does she think I take the tops off of the markers while no one is looking just for fun.

"I'm sure we have more in the basement," she yelled back instead. "I'll go check." She gave a heavy sigh. It was less work for her to go find them herself than to have Gemma go get them. Claire knew she needed to get the kids tucked into bed soon. She still had to finish getting ready for the week ahead and pay their bills.

"Come on Brita. Time to get out of the tub so I can get markers for your sister." She picked Brita up and wrapped her in a towel. "Dry yourself off and I'll be right back," she said as she put her down on the bathmat.

Claire left the room and ran down the two flights of stairs to the basement. She found a new package of markers in the extra school supply bin and ran back up the two flights of stairs. Breathing heavily as she opened Gemma's door, she tossed the markers on the floor next to her. "You forgot to knock." Gemma rolled her eyes at her.

"How about, 'thank you, Mom,'" Claire responded in a sarcastic tone.

"Thanks," she replied with little sincerity. Annoyed, Claire closed the door. She walked back down the hall and into the bathroom.

Brita was standing on the bathmat. Her hair was completely white. "Look, Mama, I'm grandma." Brita was holding the bottle of baby powder in one hand with a big smile on her face.

"Oh, Brita!" she exclaimed, shaking her head. "Patrick!" she yelled out the bathroom door. "I need you."

"What's the matter?" he yelled back from who knows where in the house.

"Again!" she said.

"Grandma?" he asked.

"Yup," she said.

"On my way."

She heard his heavy feet running up the stairs and a loud "ouch" from him as he must have forgotten to duck on the low hanging edge of the ceiling on his way up and hit his head again.

Claire scooped Brita up and put her back in the bathtub. Patrick walked into the bathroom and started laughing. "It is not funny," Claire said, swatting him with the towel and laughing herself.

"It kind of is," Patrick said as he reached over and turned the water back on.

"Look, Daddy, I'm Grandma!" Brita said to him with a huge grin on her face as she stared at her reflection in the faucet head. "I'm an old lady," she said pretending to talk with no teeth.

Patrick and Claire looked at each other and smiled. Brita, the unexpected child, who kept them entertained. She was the blessing they didn't know they needed.

"Come on, Brita. Let's get you all cleaned up." Patrick filled the bathtub back up with water.

"But I want to be Grandma, Daddy," she responded to him, shaking her white hair around sending baby powder into the air. Brita was not the name they had decided on for their little girl. In fact, they still had not decided on a name when Claire went into labor. Gemma was named after Claire's grandmother. Grayson was a name they both liked. Brita's name came by complete accident.

Claire's water broke at five in the morning. She thought she had peed herself in her sleep because it's something pregnancy can do to the body. She realized when she sat up to go to the bathroom this was more, a lot more.

"Patrick," she said, tapping him on his arm. "My water just broke."

"Okay," he said as he rolled away from her.

"Patrick, it's time." He turned his head back to her and then looked down at the bed sheets.

"Oh!" he exclaimed as he jumped out of bed and raced around the room getting dressed and grabbing the hospital bag Claire had put together. "I'll call my mom." Patrick grabbed his cell phone off the bedside table. "Hi, mom. I know it's early. I'm sorry. Yes, it's time. Her water broke. Okay, see you soon."

"She's on her way," he said, turning to her. By the time they got to the hospital, Claire had called her doctor's office and spoke with the on-call service. Her contractions had begun, and they were intense. She knew they got to the hospital, she somehow made it into a bed in the maternity ward, but she didn't remember too much as her contraction pain was the worst of her pregnancies.

"Patrick," she cried. "I hurt. Really, really bad." Claire shifted around in the bed trying to find a comfortable position between the contractions.

"I'm so sorry, babe," he said between talking to the nurse and sending a text to his mom. The nurse's name was Heidi and, no one else was more important to Claire in that moment than Heidi. People kept coming and going, but Heidi stayed by her side the whole time.

"Please don't leave me?" she begged her, grabbing the young girl's hand, not wanting to let go.

"I'm not going anywhere," Heidi reassured her, squeezing her hand gently for comfort. Heidi had the most comforting brown eyes, which helped to put Claire's anxiety at ease.

She had no idea where Patrick went, all she wanted was Heidi to be with her forever. Dr. Feldman, her OBGYN, entered the room. "Look who is right on time," he said with a smile. "She's coming on her due date and I'm the doctor on call. This little girl is punctual."

With her feet in the stirrups, and her privates exposed for the whole room to see, Dr. Feldman began examining Claire. "Ten centimeters. Looks like you are ready. Where's Patrick?"

"I...have...no...idea!" she said through gritted teeth as another contraction began, sweat poured down her forehead.

"I think he went to talk to your family in the waiting room. I'll go get him," Heidi placed a cold face cloth on her brow.

"No, please don't leave me." Claire gripped Heidi's hand even tighter, desperation in her voice.

Just then, Patrick walked in the door. "You are right on time, Daddy," Dr. Feldman said. "Your little girl is ready to make her appearance into the world." Patrick walked around the bed and held Claire's other hand.

"Are you ready for this?" Dr. Feldman asked her. Yes, she thought, get this baby out of me! I'm in pain. But she couldn't say it out loud because she was having another contraction. They were happening so close together.

Claire pushed for twenty minutes. She didn't remember as some kind of animal instinct took over and her body did what it was meant to do. She remembered sweating, crying, begging Heidi to not ever leave her, telling Patrick to stop talking. Then the sound of the cries of their little girl.

"Here she is!" Dr. Feldman said, wrapping the baby up in a blanket and handing her to the nurse next to him.

"Oh Claire, she's so beautiful!" Patrick said. "She looks just like Gemma."

"What's her name?" Dr. Feldman asked while waiting to deliver the placenta.

"Brita," she breathed out heavily and turned to Heidi with desperation in her voice. "Brita."

"Brita?" Patrick asked.

"Brita," Dr. Feldman said.

"Brita, I like it," Patrick said.

Brita was not what she planned to name her third child. She was thirsty and hot. They had a Brita water filter at home and whenever someone wanted water from the fridge, they would ask, "Can you hand me the Brita?" or "pass me the Brita." She was not telling them the name of her newborn daughter.

She was asking for water, not to name their child after a water filtration system. But Brita it was, and it somehow fit her perfectly. At least it's a good story for her to tell when she grows up.

***

After the kids were settled into bed, Claire went back to the task of paying the bills. As she sat down at the desk again, Patrick came into the room and sat in the worn-out, brown leather chair next to her. He picked up his guitar and started to strum on the strings.

"So did you figure out which bill will not get paid this month?" he asked.

"Not yet," she replied, "I hate this. It makes me so sad and depressed." Her eyes began to water. She easily cried these days and peed herself when she laughed. Another joy of three pregnancies.

"Claire, we've been through this. We need another year. We get Brita into school full-time, and we won't be so tight on money. Daycare is killing us."

"I know, I know," she said as she turned back to the computer, dreading having to deal with their finances.

Patrick and Claire assumed they were past living paycheck to paycheck. They were a two-income family. They both made a decent living. Patrick worked in IT, and she taught second grade in the same district the kids attended. Their schedules worked out great since Claire had the same vacations and summer breaks as the kids. They thought they were finally getting out of the "hole" once Grayson started attending school full-time. Then Brita was born, and they were back to paying for daycare. Claire would have stayed home with her, but her health insurance plan as a teacher was better than Patrick's. Claire carried so much guilt over their finances. She did most of the spending. Between paying the bills, grocery shopping, and buying the kids' stuff, she watched the money go out more than come in.

"I hate being in this situation. We work too hard to have to live this way," she said, turning to him with tears of frustration in her eyes.

"It's not like we are the only ones dealing with this."

"Yes, I know. I was just hoping we were past living paycheck to paycheck. We are in our mid-thirties now. It'd be nice not to have to worry about our finances so much. If we weren't still paying on both of our student loans...that extra money each month would be a huge help."

"So, what do you want me to do, Claire? Get another job. Start selling off stuff in the house. We're both on yearly salaries. We both have really good jobs. I hate having this same discussion every month when you pay the bills," he said holding his guitar but no longer playing it.

"Then you do it." Her voice was much harsher than she meant it to be.

"I would but you hate it when I do them."

"That's because you get in the worst mood after paying the bills. It's fine," she said more to comfort herself than Patrick.

"Mama, come snuggle." They both looked up at the stairs and saw Brita's little face between the spindles of the railing. They looked at each other and back at their baby girl.

"Mama is busy, I'll come snuggle with you." Patrick said as he began to put his guitar on its stand.

Claire's heart dropped. "No, I will go. Bills can wait. The kids come first." Claire stood up and made her way to the stairs.

TWO

Monday Morning, the rat race began. Each morning consisted of Brita being up before everyone and ready for the day ahead.

"Mama, Mama, wake up!" She pulled at the covers that were tucked around Claire, who hated mornings. The sun peaked in through the blinds as Claire tried to shake the sleep out of her eyes.

"Mamma, do I get to see my friends today?" Brita climbed onto their twelve-year-old queen size bed and began bouncing up and down. Claire thought at some point the mattress would collapse to the floor from Brita's daily wake-up calls.

"Yes, Brita. Today's a daycare day." Claire's eyes didn't seem to want to open quite yet to look at her daughter, but she forced a smile on her face for Brita's sake.

"Yeah," she cheered and ran out of the room.

"Grayson!" Brita yelled at the top of her lungs. "Grayson, I get to see my friends today."

As the middle child, his temperament reminded Claire of her own middle sister, Elana. Easy going, Elana got along with everyone as well. Although her sister had once told her boys were easier, Claire was not sure if it was because he was a boy or because he was the middle child.

Elana had an eighteen-year-old son, Danny, who was a gentle, old soul. He was the result of a college pregnancy and had been an amazing child since he first opened his eyes. Elana joked around saying he was her unexpected ticket out of college since she never wanted to go to college in the first place. Elana wanted to be a struggling artist living among other struggling artists in a commune. When Danny came along, he proved to be the most precious gift she could have asked for and her life shifted direction. The first grandchild had also changed her parents. They all of sudden became affectionate people.

Growing up, her parents never got on the floor and played with the girls. They weren't huggers or people to go to for comfort. That changed after her nephew was born. Claire wondered if it was because they didn't have to care for him twenty-four hours a day or because he was an easy baby. Grayson was the same as his cousin. He was comfortable anywhere and with anyone. He went with the flow. Claire often thought to herself, *Thank goodness for Grayson.*

"Babe," Claire said, poking her head up from her cocoon of blankets. She whacked Patrick on the shoulder with the back of her hand. "Time to get up."

"Uh, I hate mornings." He grumbled, throwing the floral duvet cover off his body but not making a move to get up.

"Yup, happy Monday morning." She wished for the days when she could push the snooze button ten more times before getting up.

If Claire thought Sunday nights were crazy, Monday mornings were worse. She tried to get to school early to get everything set up for the day in her classroom, but it never worked. It was not easy getting five out the door on time. She wanted to be the teacher who prepped everything the night before, but she was always so tired that by the end of the day the thought of doing one more thing exhausted her even more. She was also invariably in a time crunch to leave school to start the second half of her day, picking up Brita from daycare and running the other two to all of their after-school activities. Sometimes she felt like she should be driving a yellow taxicab instead of her old gray minivan.

She threw her side of the covers off her body which landed halfway onto Patrick. He grumbled in response. She headed into their tiny master bathroom. The sink, toilet, and shower were arm's length from each other. Claire didn't mind having a small bathroom the size of a linen closet as it meant she could have some uninterrupted time to herself when she was in there. Claire had to shower first thing in the morning, or she couldn't function. She was thankful for her straight, brown hair since she did not have to blow-dry it. A little product and it was good to go. Au naturelle was one way to save time in the morning. All the Flannigan girls had the same mousy, brown hair. Both her daughters had also inherited the family gene.

She dressed in her usual teacher uniform of jeans, dress shirt, cardigan sweater, and flats then headed downstairs to have breakfast and make the kids' lunches. "Gemma, time to get up. Get a move on!" she yelled down the hall while she walked down the creaky old stairs with the foot warn carpet down the middle.

"I'm already up!" Gemma yelled back with an annoyed tone of voice. *I think this is our relationship now. We yell at each other from other rooms and no matter what I say, I'm annoying.*

As she turned into their 1950's kitchen, which was in desperate need of a remodel, she saw that Grayson and Brita were already at the breakfast table. He had poured cereal for the two of them. *Thank God for this beautiful child.* Patrick walked in behind her and headed to the coffee maker. *How did he shower and get dressed already?* She opened the refrigerator and pulled out the ingredients for the kid's sandwiches.

Patrick poured a mug of coffee and handed it to her before getting his own. *It's the little things.* Claire inhaled the sweet aroma of her Sumatra dark roast. They had been drinking their coffee black since their first years living together when they were so broke they couldn't afford coffee and milk. Coffee was more important. She lifted the mug to her mouth and took the first morning sip of caffeine that always made everything better.

"Okay," Claire said with authority. "Here's the agenda for today. Dad is taking Brita to daycare, and I'll be picking her up."

"Yeah, friends!" she mumbled through a mouthful of cereal and milk dribbling down her chin. Claire smiled at her and continued.

"Today is our turn to carpool Gemma's theater crew. Grayson, after school, you're going over to Kyle's house until I get home, okay?" Grayson stood up from the kitchen table and brought his bowl over to the sink.

"Yeah," he said as he left his bowl and spoon in the sink.

Claire glanced at him and then the dishwasher. "Grayson, dishwasher."

Patrick reached around her and grabbed a slice of cheese from the deli bag and shoved it into his mouth then leaned over and kissed her on the cheek. "All right let's get a move on everyone. Brita and Gray head on upstairs and finish getting ready for school. Don't forget to brush your teeth," he said.

"Gemma," Claire yelled over her shoulder as she wrapped the sandwich she just made into a reusable bag. "Let's go. Your bus will be here soon."

"I'm right here," Gemma rounded the corner to the kitchen with her lips pressed together, rolling her eyes. She grabbed her lunch bag off the counter. Claire quickly took it back and put Gemma's water bottle into the side pocket and handed it back to her.

Patrick looked over at Gemma. "Nope," he said, pointing to her outfit. "Go change." Claire looked up from the mustard she was spreading onto a slice of wheat bread. She shook her head at Gemma. She didn't know why Gemma tried to push the envelope with Patrick. It didn't matter if "it's what everyone is wearing," Patrick was not ready to see his daughter looking so womanly and neither was Claire.

"Dad!" Gemma tried to pull down her short-sleeved crop top over her low-rider jeans. It didn't help that the top had a v-cut neckline showing off her blossoming figure. She took her hair out of its ponytail holder as if her long hair flowing past her shoulders would make the outfit more acceptable.

"Go." He pointed to the stairs while staring at her. Gemma knew Patrick's narrowed eyes and clenched jaw were not to be disobeyed.

"Fine," she said as she huffed out of the room. They could hear her feet stomping up the stairs.

***

Claire got to work by 8:10. Contractually, she didn't have to be there until 8:20. She took that as a win. Ten minutes early was still early. Her co-worker Greta stopped at her door. She also taught second grade in the room next door.

"Good morning," Greta said cheerfully, popping her head around the corner of the door.

"Morning." Claire was putting stacks of papers in order on her desk for her lessons that day.

"How was your weekend?" she asked as she used a lint roller to get dog hair off her shirt.

"Honestly, I don't even remember what we did," Claire replied.

"Yup, that's what happens when you have young kids," she said, tearing off a strip of lint roller paper to reveal a fresh one, and continuing to scour her shirt for any dog hair she may have missed.

Claire considered Greta her fairy godmother. Her kids were grown and out of the house, her husband was retired and played golf most days, and Greta walked around spreading pixie dust and sunshine everywhere she went. They had worked together since before Gemma was born. Claire laughed and cried and cried and laughed on Greta's shoulder many times.

"Last night was the first Sunday of the month." She glanced over at Claire. "Did you and Patrick have the money argument again?"

"Yup, same argument, different month." It was the beginning of November. Claire didn't even want to think about the upcoming holidays and how they were going to make that work.

"I'll go get the chocolate. You'll need it before the kids arrive." Greta turned out the door and towards her own classroom.

Claire adored Greta.

***

"MORNING, MRS. RHODES," THE STUDENTS ALL GREETED HER AS they shuffled their feet through the classroom door.

"Good morning," she said as they arrived, the kids sat down at their desks and started on their morning work that was displayed on the Smart Board.

Claire loved being a teacher. It wasn't just what she did for a living, it was who she was down to her core. She enjoyed seeing all their excited faces when something new clicked or they overcame an obstacle in learning that had been challenging for them.

"Today, friends, we are starting a new unit. I am so excited for this one. It's my favorite."

"You say that with every unit," a blonde-haired girl with two missing front teeth said. Claire smiled at her. She wasn't wrong.

"Look at the board and get started on your morning work if you haven't already. Grab a breakfast from the bin if you're hungry and we'll have morning meeting soon. I hope you all had a great weekend," she said enthusiastically.

She had a productive Monday with her class. The kids had two specials, music, and gym, which meant Claire had more time to prep what she didn't finish the night before. She felt prepared and ready for the rest of the week, a good way to end a Monday. She picked up her school bag and headed to her minivan with a smile on her face. It was time for her to start the second half of the day.

After picking Brita up from daycare, they headed to the grocery store. Claire had learned an easier way to go grocery shopping. She would order their groceries online and pick them up at the store. It helped her stick to a budget, and she didn't have to deal with dragging the kids through the store. This also meant she wasn't buying tons of extra stuff or spending the whole time telling her kids what they wanted to get wasn't on the grocery list.

"Thank you," she said as she waved out the window to the teenager who loaded up the trunk of the minivan. "Ready, girlfriend?" she said to Brita in the rear-view mirror. Brita had her sunglasses on her face all crooked and the elastics from her pigtails hung halfway down her head, which was a good sign of how much fun she had at daycare.

"Ready, Mama," she said with a smile and a thumbs up from the back seat.

Twenty minutes later they pulled up into the driveway. As she helped Brita out of her car seat, Claire noticed the front door was wide open. They walked over to the open door. "Why is the front door wide open," she yelled into the house. "And why are you here. And since you are, I need help with groceries,"

Grayson came running down the stairs with Kyle trailing behind him. "Hi, Mom," he said kissing her on the cheek and rubbing Brita's head.

"Hi, Mom," Kyle said as he ran past her, also rustling Brita's already disheveled hair.

Kyle and Grayson had been attached at the hip since the Rhodes family moved into the house eight years ago. They were great neighbors, and the boys had the best friendship, more like brothers than friends. Claire walked through the open front door and looked around. Their backpacks were thrown about; wrappers were all over the furniture and multiple cups were on the coffee and end tables. She sighed heavily. "Boys, one cup can be used for multiple drinks and again, why are you here? You're supposed to be at Kyle's house until I get home," she yelled disapprovingly out the door. She glanced at her neighbor's house and saw Janie, Kyle's mom, waving to her from the front step while she chatted away on her cell phone. Claire waved backed. Claire thought at some point she would need to set some rules to the revolving doors between the two houses, but for now, she was grateful for Janie keeping an eye on Grayson until she got home.

***

By Friday, Claire was barely standing. She was exhausted. She dragged herself out of her classroom and to her car feeling her energy deplete more and more with each step. She knew she drove home with Brita and walked into the house. Somehow, she ended up curled up on the couch with Brita watching *Paw Patrol.* She could hear her other two children in the house somewhere, but she kept dozing in and out of sleep until her cell phone rang.

She pulled it out of the back pocket of her jeans and glanced at the number. It was her sister, Becca. She sighed in frustration. She did not want to answer it. After Becca went away to college, they grew apart. It was like Becca went off to college and left everyone behind, especially her sisters. By the time she moved back after law school, Claire and Patrick were dating, and the sisters' once close relationship was non-existent. Growing apart had been hard for Claire; Becca was her person, her sister, her surrogate mother. Now they only spoke out of necessity.

Claire's parents, Joe and Justine Flannigan, had three daughters. Rebecca, Elana, and Claire. The three girls' personalities represented their birth order. Rebecca, or Becca, was the oldest. She was the most organized, career driven, and a perfectionist, which made getting along with her challenging, Claire thought she held high expectations for everyone. Elana, or Laney, her middle sister, had always been the free spirit, the mediator trying to keep the peace in the family. Laney's motto was *it all works out in the end.* Claire, the baby of the family, never quite knew where she fit into the mix. Most of the time she felt like an inconvenience. Her father was always working, and her mother treated her like another burden to carry.

She knew her mother grew up as an only child with absentee parents. Both of Claire's grandparents were part of the baby boomer generation. They had a strong and focused work ethic. Justine had an emotional wall built up around her only their father could get through. By the time her older sisters left for college, Claire was thirteen and moving into her formative teen years. Her mother had checked out of mothering long before that. Not much conversation happened in the Flannigan household during her middle school and high school years. She swore Laney moved three hours away, so she didn't have to deal with their family anymore. Claire closed her eyes, took a deep breath, and answered, "Hello."

"Listen, tomorrow we need to go to Mom and Dad's house and help them out with a few things to get the house ready to list. I'm going to go over there first thing in the morning. I can text you before I leave so you can meet me there." This was how all conversations went with Becca. There was no greeting. It was all business, with her telling Claire what to do, and Claire was supposed to go along with it. Her parents said it was the lawyer in her, but their father was a lawyer and had a gentle way of speaking with everyone. The sisters swore he won all his cases by killing everyone with kindness.

"Becca, I have to check with Patrick. We have things we need to get done too. The weekends are our only time to do all the household chores and the kids have to be driven everywhere." Claire could hear her sister's huffy sigh from the other end of the receiver.

"You can't expect me to do all of this by myself, Claire. Mom and Dad need our help. You know, what you need to do is let Patrick figure it out."

Claire cringed at her words. She knew Becca didn't get it. She had never been married and had no children. She didn't understand how sacred weekends were for a family. "I don't expect you to do it all by yourself, Becca. Text me in the morning." She relented to her sister. Becca hung up. *Guess that was the end of another beautiful heart-to-heart conversation between sisters.*

Claire did love her sister, but Becca didn't make it very easy to like her. Their parents were getting ready to sell their childhood home and move into a retirement community. To say they kept everything from their childhood was an understatement. Not for sentimental value, but because they never threw things away. The attic and basement were bursting with school papers and old prom dresses, boxes of Barbie dolls, and board games. Elana thought their parents should visit her, and then the other two sisters could hire people to go in and clear out the house while they were away. Sounded perfect to Claire, but their mom was under the impression the girls might want some of the furniture and other stuff. Stuff was all Claire and Patrick had in their own house. Their house was too small for all the "stuff" they already had.

She heard the sound of the garage door open, and Patrick's car pulled into its spot. She listened to the sound of the garage door close and remembered she still needed to feed her family. She knew she should get up off the couch. All she wanted was dinner to magically appear on the kitchen table, so she didn't have to move until it was time to go to bed.

"I'm home," Patrick yelled from the kitchen. She heard his keys jingle as he hung them on the key hook in the kitchen.

"We're in here." Her voice could be heard over the top of the couch. Patrick walked in and Brita jumped from the couch onto his back.

"Where's Brita? Did you forget to pick her up from daycare?" he said as Brita laughed while choking him with her little hands gripped in fists around his neck.

"I'm right here, Daddy," she said while he flipped her around and dropped her back down on the couch next to Claire.

She loved seeing Patrick with their kids. She was grateful her husband was a more involved father than her own father had been. Patrick made sure to always be home from work in time for them to eat dinner as a family. He loved going to all the kids' activities. If for some reason he couldn't make it as soon as he saw them, he'd ask them about all the details.

Patrick sat down at the end of the couch, lifting Claire's feet up so he could slide in. "How was your day, dear?" he asked sarcastically. He always knew how wiped out she was by the end of the week. They had vastly different jobs. He sat at a computer all day solving technical issues. She stood all day and instructed, directed, counseled, and mothered a classroom of twenty-three seven-year-olds.

"Becca just called," she replied with her eyes half-opened.

"And..." He picked Brita up from her perch on Claire's lap and tucked her into the small space between the two of them.

"She wants me to meet her at our parents' house tomorrow morning to start clearing it out and she wants you to 'figure out' what to do about carpooling the kids around." She emphasized with air quotes.

"Claire, you have got to say no to her. She's making so much more out of this move than it needs to be. We need to do what Laney said and call in a junk removal company."

"I agree, but if Becca isn't working then she doesn't have anything to do, and this gives her something to do." At least that's what Claire assumed. She had no idea what her sister did with herself other than work. "I also think she likes arguing with our mother."

"Then let her go over there and do it herself. The weekends are the only time we have together." Patrick leaned back to pull his phone out of his front pocket and opened his calendar app browsing through their weekend events.

"I know, I know," she said, not making eye contact because she knew she wouldn't stand up to Becca. They both knew it. Even as adults, Becca was still an authority figure for Claire.

"I'm sorry, Claire. I love your family, but they drive me crazy. They want and take, but when's the last time they offered to help?" Claire didn't say anything back. Sadly, she knew he was not wrong.

"What's for dinner?" Patrick asked, sliding his phone back into his front pocket.

"I have no idea," she said and then turned her head back to *Paw Patrol*.

***

CLAIRE KNEW HER MOTHER HAD NOT PLANNED ON HAVING ANY children, never mind three children. She had mentioned it over the years during moments of frustration. She also knew her mom wanted to marry her dad the moment she met him. She had told this to the girls on her rare moments of reflection. She said their dad swept her off her feet with his brilliant mind and gentle manner.

From what Claire knew from either stories or overhearing her mother talk, Justine wanted to have a powerful and successful career like her own mother. She had graduated from the University of Hartford with a business degree. She would repeatedly say she wanted a career so she could be important. A job where other people would come to her for advice, and she would have all the answers.

After she graduated from college, her mom worked for one of the big insurance companies in Hartford. She told the girls how depressing the job had been. That she sat at a desk all day in front of a computer. She mostly worked on liability claims and did data entry work. She said once she got pregnant with Becca, she knew she had found her way out. By that time, their father was working in a law firm and making a decent enough living to support their small family. After Becca was born, Justine became a full-time parent. She found a nice group of other stay-at-home moms and spent most days having playdates with them. The women could complain about their husbands and children together while the kids occupied each other before afternoon naptime.

Three years later, Elana was born. Their mother had two girls' eating and sleeping schedules to maintain. She wasn't the most motherly of mothers. She did not enjoy playing on the floor with them. She didn't pull them on her lap and read books to them or crawl in bed by their side when they were sick. She liked being the purpose person. She cooked their meals and made sure they had clean clothes. Her own mother had not been a hands-on mother either and she didn't feel the need to be one either. She had figured life out on her own and figured the girls would as well. At least, that was something the girls had heard often from their mom growing up.

Claire knew her mother assumed she would be able to go back to work once Elana was in school full-time. Justine had talked about that being her plan many times in front of the girls. But when Elana was in kindergarten, Justine discovered she was pregnant again. Claire was not a planned pregnancy and by that time, Justine said she found being a stay-at-home mother extremely boring. At least when it was the two older girls, they would occupy each other. When they were both in school, Justine did not know what to do with Claire. Her mother openly discussed if she was going to have to stay home longer, she might as well make money while doing it. It was during that time she decided to open her home daycare.

Justine thrived at running a daycare. The parents loved her. They came to her for parenting advice, asked about nutrition and developmental milestones. They would say to her things like "I don't know how you do it with three girls of your own" or "You're the best, Justine, thank you for all you do" or "We'd be lost without you, Justine." She ate up all of the accolades from the parents. Claire found it somewhat ironic her mother was so good at caring for other people's children, but never cared for her own.

The Flannigan girls had heard their mother say time and time again with a laugh, "I figured if I had to stay home with my girls, I could at least make some money doing it." They heard it so many times growing up they were desensitized to its true meaning. One time, when all three girls were helping their mother give a tour of the house to a potential new family, Justine said to their guests, "Becca is my oldest. She is the perfect little mommy. She takes care of her sisters while I take care of the other children. With her around, I don't have to worry about the other two. It's a win-win situation for everybody." At the time, this proclamation made Claire proud of her big sister.

Becca left for college two years later. Elana followed not long after that. Claire was left alone with their parents. She already had so many insecurities because of the way their mother treated her when her sisters were around. She constantly talked over her or ignored her unless she had a chore for Claire to do. After her sisters left for college, Claire was lonely. Her father worked long hours and wasn't around much. She became more an employee in the house than a child. Justine would leave her a list of things that needed to be done each day. She never asked her about school, her friends or even to watch television with them on the rare occasion her dad was home before she went to bed.

***

THE NEXT MORNING, BECCA TEXTED CLAIRE AT EIGHT-THIRTY saying she was leaving to head to their parents' house. Luckily, Claire had been up for a couple of hours as their alarm clock, Brita, woke them up at six o'clock asking if today was a friends day. They were both back to watching *Paw Patrol* on the couch while Claire drank her second cup of coffee snuggled up under a cozy fleece blanket.

Grayson strolled into the living room. His hair was spiked up and out everywhere and he was still wearing the same clothes he was in the day before. "Good morning," Claire said, glancing over at him.

"Morning," he mumbled as he plopped himself down into a chair and grabbed a blanket off the back of it to cover himself in.

"I'm heading over to Memes and Pops today. Do you want to come with me?" She tossed a throw pillow over at him. He caught it and hugged it into his chest, resting his head on it. Just his bedhead could be seen as he buried his face into the pillow.

"Nah. I'm heading over to Kyle's and then a bunch of us are going to the movies this afternoon. Dad said it was fine. Kyle's mom is dropping us off and Dad said he could pick us up after the movie." His words were muffled inside the pillow.

"Wow, okay. Glad you all have it planned. How about you, munchkin?" she said to Brita who had herself hanging upside down off the couch watching TV. She reached over and tickled her belly button which was sticking out of her pajama top. Brita giggled. "Do you want to come to Memes and Pops with me today?"

"Will Aunt Becca be there?" she asked, tilting her head up to look at Claire.

"Yes."

"No, she's a grumpy bird."

Claire didn't bother to correct her. *She's not wrong.*

***

Claire spent the day being directed by both her mother and sister as to what went where. Her father was hiding somewhere in the house avoiding them all. *Smart man.* They made three piles; pitch, donate, and keep. Claire thought all they accomplished was moving things from one spot to another. It was a day of getting nothing done. Her parents had lived in the blue, colonial house at the end of East Hill Road for thirty-one years. They moved in when Claire was five years old. She barely remembered living anywhere else. All their baby stuff was gone, but their mother kept everything else. She loved the memories she made with her sisters when they were kids in that house. It was the only home she'd ever known before moving in with Patrick. When her two older kids were younger, they loved coming here and playing in the sisters' old bedrooms and having sleepovers at Memes and Pop's house. Once Brita was born, the sleepovers stopped. Claire figured three was a lot to ask of them. Her parents now felt the house was too much upkeep for them. They were both ready for something smaller and simpler, but she knew it would be difficult for them to leave. They were two people who found comfort in their routines.

It was a little bittersweet to see them move. She thought about the possibility of her and Patrick buying the house from her parents as it was much bigger than their house. Now as she looked around; the wallpaper was peeling off the walls, the carpets were old and worn, it needed a new roof and siding, and trees needed to be cut back or taken down; it was too much for her and Patrick to take on. They had enough to manage with their own older home.

As she looked around at all the piles they had made that morning, she knew Elana was right. They needed to hire a junk removal company to come in. She decided to call her this weekend and tell her to schedule it. Let Elana be the bad guy and have the conversation with their mother. Elana repeatedly got away with saying and doing anything she wanted, and their mother always seemed to not have the energy to object to her.

***

As young children, Becca and Elana were Claire's people. They were the ones who hugged her when she cried, read books to her, and tucked her in at night. With their mom busy with the kids in her care, she didn't have time or patience for her girls. Becca assumed the mother role of the two younger girls. There was one memory which consistently resurfaced in Claire's mind. It was at their old house. There was an old, wooden swing set in the backyard. Claire, around four years old, was swinging on one of the plastic seats when a boy named Steven came up behind her and pushed her off so he could have a turn. Claire fell forward and scraped her knees and the palms of both hands. A thin stream of blood flowed down her leg from the cut on one knee. She began crying. Their mother yelled from across the yard, "Steven, that's not nice. Say sorry to Claire. Claire, honey, you're fine put a little spit on it." Her mother went back to doing whatever she was doing.

Twelve-year-old Becca ran over to both of them, got down on her knees and gave Claire a hug. "Steven, you may not push anyone. Ever. You ask for a turn. No more swings for you. Go play in the sandbox." Becca stood up and took Claire by the hand and led her into the house where she cleaned her knees and hands. Then she carefully put first aid cream and a Band-Aid on the cut.

The girls walked back outside. Steven was standing next to their mother crying. "What is he crying about?" Becca asked Elana. Nine-year old Elana, with a mischievous grin on her face, looked over at him and back at her sisters.

"Somehow my shovel full of sand landed on Steven's head and he got sand in his eyes. Whoops." Elana shrugged her shoulders without one ounce of guilt on her face. Becca wrapped an arm around her shoulder giving her a side hug while still holding Claire's hand. The Flannigan girls stuck together.

THREE

It was November and their parents wanted to have their house ready to list for the spring market season. There was a lot of work to be done to get it ready. Claire called Elana on Sunday afternoon to update her on the progress from the day before. Elana agreed to talk to their mother about hiring a junk removal company. Elana had always been the peacekeeper in the family. Claire knew if Elana made the call her parents would agree. She had a way with people, which was why she was a great small business owner. She ran a quaint, apothecary and gift shop on Cape Cod, The Treasure Trove. Her shop was very popular with tourists during the summer months. With that out of the way, Claire felt like she could go back to focusing on her immediate family and breathe a little.

Gemma's theater club was putting together a showcase of one-act plays, and Claire volunteered to organize ticket sales. She spent a good part of the morning creating a ticket order form from a template she found online.

Claire's mother and father were never involved in the Flannigan girls' activities when they were kids. In fact, other than driving and dropping the older two off and picking them up from activities, Claire didn't remember them doing anything school related. Her mom repeatedly said she was doing her part by taking care of other people's children all day. Their father was always working.

Becca loved to ride horses growing up and Elana was into art. When Claire was younger, her job was to sit in her car seat while her mother drove the older girls wherever they needed to go. Claire had mastered eating snacks in the car without spilling drinks or getting crumbs everywhere. As she got older, she participated in Brownies and then Girl Scouts. She was only allowed to sign up for after-school activities that happened at her school because it made carpooling easier for her mother. Not that Claire did not like being a Girl Scout, but she always wanted to try dance, gymnastics, and maybe even play an instrument. Her mother said they didn't have the time or money for it. Justine also had to work around the pick-up schedule for her sisters. So, Claire relented to being the best Girl Scout she could be she earned all the badges she could and walked the neighborhood selling boxes of cookies. Claire promised herself when she had children, she would let them explore all the activities they were interested in trying until they found what they were passionate about. She wanted her kids to have the opportunities she never got to have as a child.

Patrick's family was the complete opposite. His father, George, coached all of the boys' team sports and practiced with them in the backyard. Margie, his mother, was a stay-at-home mom who ran the bake sales, was involved in the school PTO, and hosted seasonal events at their house for the families in the neighborhood. Patrick's home was mostly male and Claire's mostly female. In the Rhodes household, Margie was the queen of her castle, and the men followed her lead. In the Flannigan household, Joe worked so much it ended up being Justine and the girls most of the time. Justine always seemed overwhelmed by her life. The girls did as much as they could to help their mother out without being asked. They did the cooking, cleaning, laundry, and played with the kids she watched. It was an unspoken rule in their house to do whatever they could to not burden their mother. When Patrick and Claire got married, bringing the two different family dynamics together was a challenge. There was a lot of trial and error to come to terms with all the personalities.

The first time Claire met Patrick's family; she went to his parents' house for dinner. After they walked through the front door, both of his parents came over to them and took turns hugging them. Claire was not used to this type of affection. Her parents were not huggers. She stood there for a moment when George hugged her and realized she was not hugging him back. She wrapped her arms around him a bit awkwardly. When it came time for dinner, they all sat down, and Margie made a toast welcoming Claire to their home. Then both parents took turns asking a million questions to she and Patrick about their lives, school, work. The conversation never stopped throughout the whole meal. His younger brother, Greg, who was tall and lanky like Patrick, came in at one point during the meal to join them and jumped right into the conversation. This was so different then dinners in the Rhodes house. Usually, it was the girls talking to each other and their mother sitting in silence unless they needed to be reprimanded for something. Their father was never home for dinner. When it was time to leave, everyone hugged again.

Once she and Patrick were engaged, they decided to introduce both sets of parents to each other over dinner at Applebee's. Claire observed her parents' response when Patrick's parents greeted them with hugs. Her parents stood rigid with their arms down by their sides. Luckily, Margie and George did not seem to notice. Margie did most of the talking throughout the meal. George did a lot of verbal agreeing to what his wife said while eating his meatloaf and mashed potatoes. Claire knew Patrick's parents' outgoing nature made her parents uncomfortable. They tried for years to get together with both sets of parents separately.

After Brita was born, the both sides decided to get together one Sunday of every month for family dinner. It made it easier for everyone to see each other with their busy schedules. It was Claire's idea. Sometimes she wondered if it was the right decision as these gatherings made her anxiety go through the roof. Their families were so different she just never knew if the conversation was comfortable for everyone or forced out of politeness. Margie did not have a filter and said whatever was on her mind. Sometimes to the point of being rude. She liked to give Claire unsolicited advice about motherhood. With her own mother, she couldn't tell if she was intimidated by Margie or just did not like her. She felt stuck in the middle to make everyone happy by trying to engage both sides with one another. She also wanted the monthly family dinners as a way of ensuring her kids got to see their grandparents, aunts, uncle, and cousins on a regular basis. She didn't grow up with family connections, but she was determined that her children would. They rotated which house hosted the monthly meal, which made it easier.

This particular month, Patrick's parents were hosting. Claire always offered to make something, but Margie liked to have complete control of her kitchen and what was served. It was best for everyone to stay out of her way. The kitchen was her domain.

They pulled into the driveway in their gray minivan, behind Patrick's brother's minivan. The rite of passage of having a family was owning a minivan. The two older kids jumped out of the car to find their cousins. Claire opened the back door and helped Brita unbuckle her booster seat. "What else needs to go in?" Patrick asked as he grabbed the flowers he insisted on stopping to buy for his mom.

"I don't think anything. She wouldn't let me bring anything, so that might be it." They walked up to the door just as Patrick's brother, Greg, came out.

"Hey guys," he said, giving Claire a half hug and patting Patrick on the back. "I'll be right back. Joss forgot the brownies in the car. I'll see you inside in a minute," he said as he headed to their car.

"Joss made brownies...unbelievable," Claire said as they stood in the doorway.

"Claire, don't. Let it go."

"What? I'm just pointing out that I offered."

"Maybe Joss just made them anyway."

Greg came back up behind them with a tray of brownies. "Were you on the fence about going in?" he said with a smile. "If not, can you let me through. Mom was adamant Joss make her famous brownies and I don't want to disappoint." Greg slid his body between them and gave Brita a kiss on the forehead as he passed by. Patrick and Claire made eye contact.

"Joss's famous brownies, right. Your mother thinks I'm incompetent in every way. She loves to tell me how I should parent our kids or where I went wrong in a recipe, even one she's never made before." The last time Margie and George hosted; Claire made corn bread pudding. Afterward, Margie texted her a recipe she had come across for corn bread pudding that *might be better if Claire ever wanted to make the recipe again.*

Patrick rolled his eyes at her and headed into the house.

Becca was the next to arrive. She waved a quick hello and headed straight to the kitchen to offer her help. Help or instruction, whichever it was, Patrick's mom loved Becca and would listen to everything she had to say. Finally, Justine and Joe showed up. They were perpetually the last ones to arrive when Patrick's parents hosted. They never seemed comfortable in Margie and George's well-kept house and modern furnishing. She could also tell they found them a bit overwhelming and preferred to keep visits short and sweet. Between seven adults and five children and all of Margie's thoughts and opinions, Claire could understand their feelings. She put on a smile and powered through these meals for her children's sake.

When they entered the living room, Claire kissed her mom on the cheek and gave her dad a hug. "Hi Mom, Dad. How's the week been? How's the cleaning out at the house going? Did the company Elana contacted show up?"

"I have never seen anything like it," her dad said. "Three men show up, Mom and I head out for the day, we come back, and it was like we drove up to a different house. Best money ever spent."

"Well, I don't know about that, but it sure was nice to not have to do all of the cleaning out ourselves. I had no idea how big our garage was.

It's been ages since we've seen the back wall." Justine walked toward the kitchen. *Don't do it.* With Becca and Margie in there, Claire would not step over the threshold unless the kitchen was on fire.

Claire yelled a quick greeting to Margie in the kitchen then headed through the dining room, out the sliding glass doors to the backyard. Brita was chasing her cousins around the two birch trees. Patrick and Claire had three kids and Greg and Joss had two, Shannon and Levi, with twins due in late spring. When the twins were born they would have four children under the age of six.

Claire's father-in-law was putting together an outdoor game for the kids. George was an easy-going man exactly like his sons. They joked around calling him "Jovial George" as he consistently had a smile on his face and a bad dad joke to tell.

"Hi George." She gave him a wave from the patio.

"Hey Claire, how goes the work?"

"It goes," she replied, grinning at him.

She walked by him and sat next to her sister-in-law. "Hey there, Mama, how are the twins treating you?"

"Well, one is sitting on my bladder making me have to pee all day and the other is up so high I have permanent heartburn. Other than that, they are good." Joss was only a couple of months along but seemed to have popped her pregnancy belly as soon as the double pink lines showed up on the pregnancy test. She was like another sister to Claire and not just a sister-in-law. She admired her so much. Joss was a strong, confident woman, who always called things exactly as she saw it in the best way. Margie had criticized her one time, and it was the last time. Joss's immediate response was, "You may not speak to me that way." Maybe that's why Margie wanted her famous brownies. Maybe it was her way of kissing Joss's ass.

The afternoon was typical. Lots of conversations over one another. Food passed around the table. Margie glared at all the children when they weren't using their best table manners. Justine and Joe kept their heads down and ate as they seemed to be counting down the minutes until they could politely leave. Claire could have given them the choice to opt out of these once-a-month family meals with Patrick's family, but she was trying to model these family traditions for her kids. She also felt like these meals meant so much to Becca as she did not have a family of her own and she got along so well with Patrick's mom.

Another family dinner was complete, and Claire could go home being able to check off the "see family" box on her monthly mental to-do list. She knew she should make more of an effort to create a relationship with her parents and sister now that she was an adult. Yet so much time had passed she didn't know how to, in her mind, this was her way of making that effort.

FOUR

Thursday afternoon came, Brita was on the floor next to Claire building a skyscraper "to the moon" with her magna tiles when Patrick walked in from work. Claire was working on her email to Gemma's school with the theater club ticket flyer attached.

"Here are my girls," he said, coming over and kissing the top of Brita's head and then leaning down to kiss Claire.

"Hey babe, how was work?" Claire said, meeting his eyes before retuning back to the computer screen.

"Well...I got some good news and not so good news." His voice sounded funny, which caused a red flag to go up in Claire's mind.

"*Okay.*" She turned to look at him. She could feel her heart jump in her chest as she got a sick feeling in her stomach. "Please tell me you didn't get laid off."

"No...no...nothing like that. We should wait until after the kids go to bed to talk about it though." He was acting very odd, barely making eye contact with her. Claire didn't like it at all.

"Yeah, no. You can't do that to me. You need to tell me now." Her voice shook with nerves as she spoke.

He grabbed her hand and pulled her out of the desk chair. He led her over to the couch. They each sat down on a cushion side by side. He was still holding her hand in his. Claire could feel her heartbeat quicken. Ideas of what could be coming flashed through her mind. He got fired, a pay cut, they had to relocate, he had cancer, he's dying, she's dying, and the doctor's called him at work.

"A new division is being opened outside of Chicago and, today, I was asked if I would be interested in leading the team to set up the office and install their new software system." His voice carried a tone of excitement and nervousness to it.

"Oh, well, that's fine," she said dismissively. "You've done that stuff before. God, Patrick, you had me worried," she let out the breath she had been holding. She also let go of his hand she had been tightly squeezing.

"The thing is..." He paused before continuing. Claire hated it when someone said 'the thing is' because the 'the thing is' was usually bad news. "Here's the good news, it would be a promotion for me. I would be the leader on the team which means a bump in my pay..."

"Babe, that's amazing!!" she said excitedly, interrupting his sentence and hugging him.

"Enough where we wouldn't feel like we were living paycheck to paycheck anymore."

"Really, oh my goodness. Like enough of a bump that I won't have a complete meltdown every month while paying bills?" she asked, bouncing up and down a little on the couch. He shook his head yes with a tentative smile and she leaned over and hugged him again. He pulled her arms down and looked her in the eyes while holding hands in his own.

"Claire, the bad news is...I have to lead the team from Chicago," he said somberly.

"Wait, what? We have to move to Chicago! What about the kids and school and my job?" She felt her palms start to sweat and tears formed in her eyes. She let go of his hands, wiping her palms on her jeans.

"No, babe, I'm saying this all wrong. Let me start again. I was offered the position to lead the IT department for the new division opening in Chicago. It would mean more money for us, but I have to do it from

Chicago. I would be working there all week and then come home on the weekends." He looked her in the eyes to make sure she understood what he was saying. Then, it clicked, and her eyes grew wider. He quickly added, "It's a one-year contract. By the time the contract ends, Brita will be attending school full-time, and we won't have to pay for daycare anymore."

"You would be gone all week. Every week? In Chicago? And I would be here, by myself? With three kids? Doing all the things?" She swept her arm around the room for emphasis landing her eyes on the pile of laundry, not folded sitting in the basket next to the couch.

"Yes, and I know it will be hard, but financially for us this is huge; and for my career, it's a step up the ladder for the possibility of more promotions. If I make this launch successful, more chances may come my way in the company." He eagerly looked at her hoping she would see the opportunity this meant for their family like he did.

"But I would have to do all the carpooling, cooking, cleaning, care for the kids, and everything by myself, all week long. Every week. Our family would be apart." She sat stunned, wringing her hands in her lap. Tears fell from her eyes. She stood up and started pacing around the room. Her heartbeat sped up as a flash of the empty bedroom she shared with Elana came to mind after Elana had left for college. While pacing the floor, Claire accidentally bumped into Brita's skyscraper, almost knocking it down.

"Mama!" Brita looked up at her in annoyance.

"Sorry, sweet pea." She shook the image out of her mind's eye and looked down at the skyscraper but did not really see it. She paced behind the couch and chair in a fog. Patrick stood up and walked over to her. Claire held her hand up like a stop sign.

"We won't have to worry about our monthly bills anymore, Claire. We can pay them all! And we can ask our family for help. My parents, your parents, your sister, my brother." She looked over at him like he had lost his mind.

"Are you kidding me?" she said, flabbergasted. "Your mother thinks

I'm the most incompetent person on the planet, and your brother and Joss have two kids of their own, and she's pregnant with twins. My parents are trying to get their house ready to sell. On top of that they could barely manage raising us girls, forget about helping raise their grandkids. You can forget about Becca. She is too busy with her career."

"My mother does not think you're incompetent. I know it seems impossible, but maybe we are not giving our family the benefit of the doubt. They might rise to the occasion. I'll do whatever needs to be done on the weekends to make the weekdays easier for you," he said. She looked at him. He had a look of hope and longing on his face. Claire closed her eyes, grabbed the bridge of her nose, and sat back down on the couch.

"I need time to process this, okay?"

"Okay," he said. "I promise, Claire. We'll make it work. It'll be okay." He leaned down and kissed the top of her head. *Easy for him to say. He'll be halfway across the country living it up in corporate housing while I'm in Connecticut managing three kids, a full-time job, and all the household responsibilities. Although, it would be nice not to have to worry about their bills each month.*

"One year?" She looked up at him with resolve in her eyes.

"One year. Again, I will do everything when I'm home to make weekdays easier for you and the kids. Even give you some free time to yourself." She grabbed his hand and pulled him down next to her. Patrick drew her into a comforting hug.

***

"WELL, THAT SOUNDS HORRIBLE," ELANA SAID FROM THE OTHER end of the phone. Claire sat in the teacher's lounge at work with Greta next to her and Elana on FaceTime. Greta and Elana had become friends through Claire and social media. The three of them tried to get together every Friday morning before school for some coffee talk and vent about their week with Elana joining them in over FaceTime when she could.

"Oh Claire, you need to go into this strategically. Make a list of what you are going to need help with, invite everyone over for lunch. Then ask who can help with what. Don't give anyone an option to not do their part. You and Patrick are always helping everyone. Now it's your turn," Greta said reassuringly. Greta had a way of saying things which made Claire feel more confident than she actually was when it came to her family. *Yes, it is my turn. They can all help me this time.*

"She's right, Claire. You can't cower if anyone says they have other things to do. Make it not an option. Make it 'how are you going to help your nieces/nephew/grandchildren.' Guilt trips go a long way with our family. Think about how Mom acted growing up and how many times she pulled the 'poor me' act with us." Elana dramatically threw her arm across her forehead. "Joe works all the time. I am home caring for our three girls. Pity me, I am a saint." Claire and Greta laughed at her dramatization of Justine. "Find your inner Becca. Make a list of what you need help with, assign the jobs out and don't take no for an answer."

She knew they were right. Claire had not been good at asking for help. When she was little, she always felt like she was a burden if she asked her parents for anything. Which was why she always went to her sisters. Claire was not a planned pregnancy, so she was not considered in the family's plans. She was a last thought being dragged along everywhere her parents or sisters needed to go, never asking for anything. If she did ask for anything—a playdate with a friend, a trip to the playground—each time her mother made the excuse they didn't have the time.

Claire knew to make this work she and Patrick would need some added support. She needed to get over her childhood insecurities and feelings of being an inconvenience so she could think about what was best for her own kids. She wanted the transition to be smooth and to keep their kids' lives exactly as they knew it.

***

THANKSGIVING WAS LESS THAN A WEEK AWAY AND PATRICK AND Claire decided it was the right time to announce his new position. To make it a celebration. Something they could be grateful for. It was Thanksgiving after all.

The kids were already tucked into their own beds. Claire and Patrick were sitting side-by-side on their bed, leaning against the pillows that were propped up against the headboard. Claire sat cross-legged with a legal pad in front of her and a pencil behind her ear. Patrick was beside her with Grayson's indoor soccer schedule, Gemma's theater schedule, and the family calendar in front of him.

"The month of December, Grayson has soccer practice Tuesdays and Thursdays and games on the weekends which I'll be home to take him to. Gemma has rehearsal Monday through Thursday after school. Rehearsal ends at five o'clock and then moves to six o'clock." Patrick read off from both schedules. "I leave for my first trip on December fourth."

Claire tried not to let her anxiety build in her throat. December was a crazy month between school functions and holiday shopping. She glanced over at Patrick and saw how hard he was trying to make this work for all of them. Patrick filled in the different days and times on the calendar. Claire had to rethink how she was going to process this change. She could either embrace the benefits of his new position or she could resist it and be miserable. Listening to her mother complain constantly about her father's work schedule played like flashes in her mind. Not wanting to take after her mother, she chose to embrace the change.

"This won't be so bad then. I'll put a taxi light on the top of the van and turn the yellow light on after work." She smiled at him, making light of the situation while leaning her head on his shoulder.

Patrick gazed over at her, placing a hand on her knee while he leaned his head on top of hers. He carried guilt in his eyes. She did not want him to feel this way. "Again, we can see if the family can help with some of the carpooling to help you out. Someone could help with driving Gemma or Grayson on Tuesdays and Thursdays. Maybe you can get out of carpool for play practice so you can come home after picking up Brita and not go back out again. We'll keep ordering groceries to be picked up and I can help with laundry and the house when I get home on the weekends, like we do now."

"Patrick, it's all going to work out." She reached down and squeezed his hand on her knee. "The weeks are so busy. They will fly by fast and then you'll be home for our family time on the weekends. We'll make it work. We always make it work." She tilted her head up and gave him a kiss. She wasn't sure if she was trying to convince him or herself.

***

THE TELEVISION BLARED FROM THE LIVING ROOM. THERE WERE children's bodies flying everywhere. No, it was not a war zone. It was Thanksgiving in the Flannigan house. Joe and Justine were hosting this year as they were expecting it to be the last Thanksgiving in the home they raised the girls in. Claire was trying hard to stay in the moment and not think about the conversation she and Patrick were planning on having with their family after dinner.

With each room she walked through, she couldn't help but notice the little reminders of childhood memories: the doorway Becca smacked her head on when she was giving the girls piggyback rides in the house. There was still a dent from her head which was a running joke in the family as to how hardheaded she was. The orange stain on the ceiling from when all the kids were playing with slime at the kitchen table and Elana decided to see if it would stick to the ceiling if she tossed it up there. It did. Their mother had to scrape it off with a metal spatula. The many secret hiding spots the girls had discovered playing hide-and-seek in the house. Running down the stairs on Christmas morning to see all the presents from Santa under the tree. Easter egg hunts in the backyard. Crawling into Becca's bed at night. Telling silly stories under the covers. Becca and Elana arguing over the bathroom so they could do their hair and make-up for school. With Claire being the youngest by eight and five years respectfully, she often felt like a spectator of her sisters' lives. She was always excited for the time when she got to do all the grown-up things they were doing.

After taking a nostalgic tour of the house, Claire walked back into the kitchen to help her mother chop vegetables for the stuffing. She walked in and gave her mother a half hug from the side; her mother's body stiffened. "What was that for?" Justine asked, sauteing onions and celery.

"I can't believe this is the last Thanksgiving in this house. Does it make you sad at all?"

"Of course, it does. I wouldn't have even considered selling it if it weren't for how bad your father's and my arthritis is. It's getting harder and harder for us to care for the house. I am looking forward to a fresh start as well. A smaller garden, someone else to mow the lawn for Dad. A retirement community does sound nice at this point in our lives."

"Well, I'm happy for you both." Her mother didn't respond. Claire knew how difficult change was for Justine. She was hoping she would share more of how she felt about the upcoming move. Claire knew her mother had trouble expressing her emotions. She wished they could share in some nostalgic moments together about the house. Instead, Justine got busy with her preparations.

After a very noisy dinner and way too much food, Patrick and Claire cleared the table. "Should we tell everyone about my new position over dessert?" he whispered while carrying a tower of plates and silverware to the kitchen.

"Yeah, that's what I was thinking." Claire walked behind him carefully carrying glassware in both hands.

They both headed over to the sink to rinse off the dishes and load the dishwasher. This was where her family came in at these meals. They were the cleanup crew. It sort of happened over the years. Claire didn't mind as it kept her from having to make small talk. She loved her family but found these holiday dinners draining. Everyone was always talking over each other, disagreeing on one topic or the other, and children were constantly being reprimanded for doing something wrong. As a teacher, this is what she dealt with all week long; she needed a break from it on the weekends and holidays. Families could be so much crueler than kids, trying to disguise it as teasing. At least kids were honest. They called it like they saw it. Most of the time, they were not intentionally trying to be mean.

After they finished washing the dishes that didn't go in the dishwasher, Patrick and Claire looked at each other. "Ready?' he asked. She nodded to him. They walked into the living room where everyone was gathered for dessert and whatever sporting event was on the television.

"Hey everyone," Patrick began, "Claire and I wanted to share some exciting news with you." He stuck his hands in his front pockets, rocking back and forth on his heels. This was his tell when he was nervous.

"You're not pregnant again, are you?" his mother asked, a frown on her face.

"No, Mom." He could hear Claire breathing heavily in frustration at his side. "I got a promotion at work. I will be overseeing the set up for the IT department for our new division opening outside of Chicago."

"That's great, son," George said walking over to him, clapping him on the back.

"Oh, Patrick. I'm so proud of you." Margie beamed.

"In Chicago?" Becca asked. "So, you'll be setting up a new office in Chicago from Connecticut. How will that work?" Claire could feel Becca's eyes boring down into her. She didn't turn her head to make eye contact. The last thing Claire wanted was to see the judgmental glare from Becca.

"No, not exactly," Patrick replied as he cleared his throat. Claire could feel the tension between her sister and her husband.

"Wait, are we moving to Chicago?" Gemma looked up from her cell phone and then from one parent to the other with her mouth agape.

"Dad, I don't want to move to Chicago," Grayson said with sadness in his voice. In hindsight, Claire realized they should have sat the kids down and explained everything to them first. Epic parent fail.

"No, no, you guys. We are not moving. I will be going to Chicago, and you will stay here." This was not going as they had planned. The scenario they created in their minds was a lot more positive.

"How's that going to work then?" his brother asked, putting an arm around his wife's shoulder, like their family dilemma was contagious and would infect his family.

"Claire and the kids will stay here, and I will fly to Chicago on Monday mornings and come back Friday afternoons. It's not permanent. Just for one year, until the new division is on its feet."

Becca watched Patrick as he spoke, and Claire watched her from the corner of her eye. She could see Becca's lawyer hat slowly slip onto her head. Her facial expression turned stern. "What you are saying is you will be leaving my sister to care for your three children all week long and work a full-time job, while you are halfway across the country?"

Yup, pretty much. Thank you for calling it out. Claire's heart began to beat faster in her chest as she knew the second half of the announcement was coming next. She was not looking forward to it.

Patrick put a big fake smile on his face before he said, "Yes, and that's where you all come in. We are hoping our family will be able to help Claire and the kids out while I'm away." Not how they had discussed presenting it. They discussed introducing it as an opportunity to spend individual time with the kids, get involved more in their activities, and help their family out. All she heard was "help Claire out."

"Honey, how do you expect us to do that? Joe and Justine are getting ready to move, your brother and Joss have their own family to take care of, and twins on the way. Becca has a very demanding job, and Dad and I have our own lives," her mother-in-law said emphatically. She glanced around the room as if everyone would be shaking their head in agreement with her.

"Unbelievable. I'm sorry Patrick, but it all sounds a little selfish of you," Becca said. Claire could see Patrick's ears turning red.

"We'll help out anyway we can," Joss chimed in, sitting up tall in solidarity with Claire and Patrick.

"Of course, we will," said Greg skeptically while rubbing his pregnant wife's back.

Mama bear mode began to set in. Claire began to talk, her voice shaking. "Thank you all, it's okay, though. Really. The kids and I will be fine. I may need some help transporting them to activities, but I'm sure I can figure out carpooling with some of the other moms." Claire hated asking for help and wished her family would offer it without making it seem like she and the kids were a huge inconvenience to their lives. An all-too-familiar feeling of abandonment washed over her. She swallowed the tears wanting so desperately to rise to her eyes. Here she was as an adult still fading herself into the backdrop. The worst part was Patrick's family was part of it now too. The Flannigan family trait metastasized to the Rhodes family. Her parents said nothing.

She looked over at Patrick and then to Gemma and Grayson. "We'll be fine, really. It's going to be an adjustment. We'll manage. The extra money will be a tremendous help and it's a fantastic opportunity for your dad. Also, it's only a year. By the time the project is over, Brita will be going to school full-time. Can you believe it? The thought of our little one in school like her brother and sister." She reached over to squeeze Brita. "Boy, time does fly." She was making light of the situation to avoid conflict. Her mom finally decided to speak.

"Claire will be fine. Joe worked all the time; I managed the three girls on my own while working full time. Look how great they turned out." Claire and Becca finally made eye contact across the room. They turned out great because the Flannigan girls took care of each other. It was one thing they could agree on.

FIVE

Claire knew whenever Becca needed to process a situation or talk things through, she texted Elana. Texting was much easier for Becca as it was one step removed from having to truly express her feelings. Elana had told Claire that once they reached adulthood, she always felt like she was in the middle of her sisters, the one to talk them through their problems with each other so they didn't have to talk to each other. Ever since Elana moved to Cape Cod, she said she didn't mind so much. She had said now that there was distance between her and her family, it made it easier carrying this role in the family. She felt connected without feeling smothered by family drama. Claire hated that Elana had to be in the middle of her relationship with Becca, but she just didn't know how to connect with their older sister like she did when they were younger.

Claire missed how close they all were when they all shared a bedroom. When Becca was moved out of the girls' shared room at thirteen, it changed the dynamic of their relationship. Whenever Claire or Elana were scared in the night, they crawled into Becca's bed. She was the big sister, the mommy of the three. After the move, Becca began to withdraw into herself. Claire was six at the time, still little.

Claire remembered sitting on her bed sandwiched between Elana and Becca. Their father and a neighbor were moving Becca's bed into their dad's old office. She asked their mother, "Why does Becca have to leave? I don't want her to leave."

"Because she's a woman now. Elana is still with you. You'll be fine." Why did grown-ups always say that? *You'll be fine.* How did they know if you'd be fine? All Claire knew was that her heart hurt for Elana and for herself. Claire clung to Becca, hoping she could keep her in their room if she held on tight enough.

This was the point in her life where Claire started to feel abandoned but not just by Becca, but both her sisters. Elana tried to fill the hole that Claire needed. But as Elana got older, she started spending more time out of the house with friends than at home with her little sister as most teenagers did. Becca still took on the mothering role for both of them, but it became harder for her because she wanted to be a teenager and have of life of her own. Claire was still young and needed her big sisters.

Claire was still in elementary school at that time. They were at various stages in their lives. When they were younger, they all felt an absence from their mother and father and bonded together. But then as they got older, they began to neglect each other. Claire was left on her own. Claire and Elana were able to keep some semblance of a friendship, but Becca and Claire were never able to gain that in their adult years.

***

AFTER THE THANKSGIVING DEBACLE, CLAIRE AND PATRICK SAT the kids down and went over the plans they made for managing the new routine. Patrick sat in the accent chair while Claire sat on the floor at his feet with the calendar they had created the previous week on the coffee table in front of her. "This is crazy," Gemma said. "You're going to be gone all week long. Who's going to wake me up in the morning? Who's going to pick me up after rehearsal from school?" *Typical teenager worried about how the change will affect her first.*

"Gemma, your world is not going to change. I will wake you up in the mornings. I am also planning on working out carpooling with the other theater moms for you on Tuesdays and Thursdays when I have to drive Grayson to soccer." Claire tried to reassure her daughter. Gemma rolled her eyes and crossed her arms at her chest. She was sitting on the couch next to her brother and sister. Brita didn't understand what was happening. She just liked being sandwiched between her siblings. Her little feet dangled off the edge of the couch as she bounced them up and down.

"I'll be gone all week, but I'll be home early Friday night. We'll still do our family time on the weekends. I'll be able to go to all your soccer games, Grayson. What do you think, buddy?" Patrick addressed Grayson.

"Sure. Whatever you have to do." Grayson shrugged his shoulders. It was hard for Claire and Patrick to get a read on him. He sat in his usual slouched posture looking like he was counting down the minutes until he could go to his room to play his video game.

"Well, I think." Brita chimed in and then looked at her parents with contemplation. "Daddy, you're going away for work?"

"Yes, sweet pea."

"But then you're coming back?"

"Every weekend. I'll be gone while you're at school with your friends. I'll call you every night to talk to you about your day and then I'll be home for dinner on Friday. Okay?" Patrick talked directly to Brita but was saying it to all three of them.

"Okay." Brita nodded dramatically.

Patrick looked down at Claire, placing a reassuring hand on her shoulder and then moved his eyes across to all three of their kids. "We are a family, and we take care of each other. We are going to need all three of you to help out around here. Clean up after yourselves, put your dishes in the dishwasher, keep your rooms picked up. I know I can count on you guys to do your part while I'm gone." The two older ones nodded yes. Brita looked up at her siblings and copied them.

"Are we good now? Can we go up to our rooms?" Gemma asked with a bored look on her face, arms still crossed at her chest.

"Yes, thank you, guys. We're the Rhodes family. We stick together, right?" Patrick said, trying to put some oomph in his voice. The older two gave him a sound of agreement. They got up from the couch and walked up the stairs. Brita slid off the couch. She hugged both of them and then followed her siblings upstairs.

"Well, that's done." Claire sighed heavily. "I love that you expect the kids to do things that they never do now." She laughed at him, patting him on the knee. "Clean up their rooms, put dishes in the dishwasher. You are a dreamer, Mr. Rhodes."

He picked her up off the floor and brought her onto his lap. He gave her a big bear hug while smothering her with kisses. They both laughed. Claire knew things were going to change. She also knew she and Patrick were a great team and would figure it out. There was a feeling of fear in the pit of her stomach that she was going to lose her family. Her past childhood trauma was beginning to surface, and she did not like the feeling of insecurity creeping up on her. Was she going to be left alone again? But this was Patrick. He was the one person she knew would always be there. The one person who vowed to always be by her side.

***

Two Mondays later, Patrick left on his first flight for his new position. He was gone before Claire and the kids woke up. Their new routine began at five-thirty in the morning. Nothing about that Monday morning was routine. As much as she prepared the night before, it was complete chaos. Claire woke up before her usual alarm clock, Brita. She showered and got dressed all by six a.m. Brita came into the room. She jumped on the bed, bouncing up and down. They said good morning and Brita raced out of the room to wake up Grayson. As Claire went to head downstairs, she remembered Gemma.

Claire leaned around the staircase corner yelling down the hall to

Gemma. "Gem, you need to get a move on, it's 6:20. The bus will be here in twenty-five minutes." No response. She walked down the short hallway to her bedroom door. "Gemma, come on you're going to be late." She opened the door and found Gemma still in bed sleeping. Claire forgot Patrick usually did the initial wake up while she was in the shower. Like Claire, Gemma was not a morning person. "Gemma," she whispered as she walked over to the bed. "Honey, you need to get up. It's 6:20. I don't want you to miss the bus."

Gemma's eyes popped open, and she jumped to a sitting position. "What! Are you kidding me? Why didn't you wake me? I'm never going to make the bus. Mom, what the hell!"

"Hey! I forgot that Dad woke you first. Of course, you will make the bus. This is our first morning. I'll remember for tomorrow. Just get up and get moving." Gemma flung the covers off herself, yelled at Claire to please leave so she could get ready, and that exchange set the tone for the rest of Claire's day.

She didn't get to school early since she had to drop Brita off at daycare and misjudged the time. She rushed into her classroom with her school bag on her shoulder at the same time as her students were walking through the door. She forgot about their monthly assembly happening first thing that morning. The art teacher was absent, and there was no sub, so art was canceled, and she lost that planning time. Claire had planned on using that time to prep her afternoon lesson because she didn't get a chance to do it the night before.

She was so frazzled by the end of the day she forgot it was her turn to carpool Gemma's friends from the theater club. She picked Brita up and began driving home. She got a very irate call from Gemma that she forgot them, and she was the worst ever. At the next intersection, she turned the van around and went to the school and picked them up. Brita was the only one excited because she loved all the attention from Gemma's friends. After dropping off the three girls to their houses and apologizing to each mother out the window, they headed home. By the time they got there, everyone was starving. Claire couldn't remember if she ate her lunch or not. Grayson ran through the kitchen door, coming from Kyle's house, he dropped his backpack next to the kitchen table. "I'm starved. What's for dinner?"

"I am too and I'm not sure. Give me ten minutes," she said as she dropped her school bag off her shoulder onto the kitchen floor.

"You got it," he said and grabbed an apple off the counter and ran out of the kitchen and headed up the stairs to his room, forgetting his backpack. Claire opened the freezer door and looked inside. Chicken nuggets and French fries it was. *I need to do better. Tomorrow, starting tomorrow. It will be much better. This is just a learning curve.* She gave herself a pep talk while preheating the oven.

Lying in bed that night, her cell phone rang, she looked at the flashing name. It was Patrick. She reached over to her bedside table and grabbed her phone, knocking a dirty tissue and the book she was reading onto the floor.

"Hey babe," she answered in exhaustion, while trying to pick up the items off the floor at the same time. She almost fell off the bed.

"Wow!" came Patrick's voice. "You sound just as tired as I feel."

"I am."

"It was that bad?" he asked. She didn't want him to feel guilty so, of course, she fabricated the truth.

"No, just a Monday. We're fine. How was your first day?" She put the tissue and book back on the bedside table and settled back into her covers, fluffing the pillow under her head with her free hand.

"The plane ride was good. I was able to get a lot of work done. I got here around nine and headed right to the office. Their systems are a mess right now, but I guess that's why they brought me in. It's going to be a ton of work. We'll get it done though. I have a good team collaborating with me."

"That's good to hear." She tried to stifle a yawn.

"Did I miss the kids? Are they still up?"

"Gemma and Grayson probably are, Brita is already asleep."

"Can I say hi to them?"

"Of course. Hold on. I'll get them." Getting them meant Claire had to get out of bed, which she really did not want to do. She pulled the covers off, trying not to moan as she left her warm spot. Grayson's room was next to theirs. She knocked on his door.

"Yeah," he said.

"Dad's on the phone and wants to say hi." She walked her cell phone across the room to him, stepping over minefields of clothes strewn across the floor. "When you're done. Please give it to your sister." She walked through the maze of his room and back to her bed, dropping herself back into her cozy spot. She must have fallen asleep as she didn't remember Gemma bringing her phone back. The next thing Claire heard was her alarm going off on the phone with the most ear-piercing sound. Claire was so used to Brita waking them up, she forgot how annoying a cell phone alarm could be.

Tuesday and the rest of the week was not much better for Claire and the kids. Claire felt like she was chasing her tail each day. She had to plan her classes' holiday celebration and meet with her room parents. Gemma and her theater club would be adding more time to their rehearsal schedule in preparation for their one-act play performances. She still had not figured out transportation for Tuesdays and Thursdays when indoor soccer began. Patrick's flight got delayed on Friday, and he didn't make it home until almost nine that night. Claire fell asleep in Brita's bed while reading her a bedtime story.

"Hey," Patrick whispered as he bent down and kissed her forehead.

"Hi," she said tiredly as she opened her eyes.

"Sorry about the delay." He brushed a lock of hair out of Brita's face.

"Not your fault. You have no control over that."

"I know. I just feel bad with it being my first week away and all."

"It's all good. Hold on, let me slide my arm out from under her and we can go downstairs and chat." Claire slowly moved her arm trying not to wake Brita. She followed Patrick down the stairs and into the living room. They sat in their usual spots on the old couch.

"So, how was it?" he asked.

"Busy, but we managed. I'm just really tired." She looked at up him. "I missed you." Patrick pulled her in closer to him giving her a gentle kiss on the lips.

"I missed you, too and I'm sorry." She pulled away to meet his eyes. She could see sorrow in his eyes over not being there to help her. She felt bad for him. She knew how much he loved being an involved dad, like his father was.

"Don't be. We'll get into our routine and figure it out." She leaned in for a deeper kiss. She wasn't sure if she said it to reassure him or herself. She was just happy to have him by her side.

They had a nice weekend, just the five of them. The weather was predicted to have off and on rain showers, but the rain held out. Claire and Patrick took the kids for a bike ride on the bike trail in town. Claire beamed the whole day. She was so proud of how her family was managing this new change to their lives. After the bike ride, they went bowling, picked up pizza, and had a family movie night. There was minimal arguing over the movie selection, which was a pleasant change. It was a perfect Saturday for Claire. Sunday was the day to get the household chores done. There was laundry to do, cleaning, lesson planning for the week ahead, and making sure the kids had everything they needed for school. Indoor soccer season was starting soon for Grayson, and Claire was able to get all that paperwork filled out. Soccer...another thing she would have to fit into the schedule. She realized this was her new norm and she had to get used to it.

***

"Uh, you're so annoying," Gemma screamed from upstairs.

"I'm not annoying. You're annoying," Grayson yelled back.

"Why can't I just have my own bathroom. This house sucks. It's too small and there are too many people in it." Claire could hear Gemma screaming as she stomped back to her bedroom and slammed the door.

"What is going on?" she yelled from the kitchen. It was Thursday night, and they always had breakfast for dinner on Thursdays. Claire was whipping the eggs in a bowl trying to ward off a headache that had been building up all day.

"Gemma is taking forever in the bathroom, and I need to go." Grayson's voice carried from across the hallway, down the stairs and into the kitchen.

"I was here first, and he can go to your room or downstairs." Gemma's voice followed.

"You're not even using it. You're just staring at the pimples on your face in the mirror."

"What? I can't believe you just said that to me. I am not." Grayson was right, she was probably counting the pimples on her face and examining them. Something she could have done in her bedroom. Claire didn't bother to point that out to Gemma.

"Can you both please stop screaming at each other? Grayson, just come down here or use my bathroom." Claire was trying to flip a pancake while yelling.

"Why do I always have to be the one to move?" Because he was the easier of the two and she didn't have it in her to fight with Gemma. Her head already hurt enough.

"Mama." Brita pulled on the hem of her shirt. "Look, Mama, I'm helping make dinner." Claire looked down and saw Brita. She had a bowl on the floor and was dumping a box of pancake mix into it. Powder was going everywhere. In the air, in her hair, all over the floor.

"Oh, thank you, honey," she said as she grabbed the box out of her hand. No point in that as it was completely empty. Claire handed Brita a spoon to mix it. She was going to have to clean up the mess anyway. Might as well let this keep her busy for a while. Claire wiped her forehead with the back of her hand and smeared pancake mix on herself. *Come on, Claire, you can do this.* She gave herself an internal pep talk.

***

"You guys, I can't do this," she said to Elana and Greta the next morning. They were having their Friday morning check-in. Claire and Greta were sitting at a table in the teacher's lounge with Elana face staring back at them. Claire had her cell phone propped up on some books so Elana could see them both. "There is not enough coffee in the world to wake me up this morning."

"Honey, be kind to yourself," Greta said. "It's only been three weeks."

"Three weeks? It seems like an eternity already. These days are so long, and I have to do this for a whole year," she said. "I am really struggling today. Patrick had to leave Sunday night for an early work meeting Monday morning. I did all the weekly prep by myself and paid bills. The extra money is already helping, so I know I shouldn't complain. I'm just so tired." She laid her head down on her hands.

"Claire, you don't have to do this by yourself," her sister chimed in from the tiny screen.

"But I do, Laney." She picked her head up to make eye contact with her sister.

"Honey, you don't," Greta said, putting her hand on top of Claires. "Just ask for help. You know we all will help anyway we can."

"Patrick and I tried at Thanksgiving and got complete pushback. It was like a 'how dare you ask' from my mother-in-law. My brother-in-law and sister-in-law have enough on their own plates, our parents are moving, and Becca is busy with work. Laney, you live three hours away. I know it sounds like I'm making excuses for everyone. I'm just having a moment. I'll be fine. I'll get over it." she said with her head only slightly lifted off her hands this time. "Do I have to go teach a room of students now?" She dropped her head back down on her hands.

SIX

Claire arrived home around four-thirty with Brita in tow and about five bags hanging off her shoulders and arms. She walked through the front door to the sounds of loud music coming from the kitchen and voices laughing. As tired as she was, all this noise just warmed her heart. The work week was over, and she could turn her teacher brain off for a couple of days and focus on her family. She walked through the living room into the kitchen to find Patrick, Gemma, and Grayson at the counter and all the ingredients for homemade pizza on the kitchen island.

"You're home?" she asked looking at her husband through loving eyes. Seeing him there made her realize how much she missed him.

"I flew in on the red eye last night. I didn't tell you because I wanted it to be a surprise. I was hoping to be home in time to see everyone before they left for school. Unfortunately, that didn't happen, but it gave me time to get things done around the house before everyone got home. The laundry is all done." Patrick looked so proud of himself. Claire couldn't help but smile at how happy he looked surrounded by their children in their kitchen.

"Dad picked up stuff for pizza night," Grayson said with a wide grin.

"Wow, very nice," she said, walking around the counter. She wrapped her arms around Patrick pulling him into a huge hug. When they came out of the hug he bent down and kissed her. Brita pulled at his pant leg, a cue she wanted to be picked up. He reached down to her, and she jumped into his arms then reached for a slice of pepperoni.

"How you doing?" Patrick asked Claire in a horrible "Joey from *Friends*" accent.

"I'm better now. I love having you home earlier." Claire was so grateful to see him. This was a tough week, and she needed her rock by her side. She and Gemma had been butting heads each morning over her outfit choices and her students were starting to get holiday vacation fever. She struggled to get anything accomplished at home or at work.

"Yeah, I love being home earlier too." He leaned across the counter and grabbed two pieces of pepperoni, one for her and one for him, and put one into her open mouth before he ate his own.

"Hey Dad, soccer orientation starts tomorrow. Are you going to take me?" Grayson asked while rolling out his pizza dough on the counter that was covered in flour.

"Of course, buddy. I'll be there." Claire could see the pride in Patrick's face as he talked to Grayson. He loved being involved with the kids' activities like his dad was for him and Greg.

"Don't forget about my rehearsal too. We are working at the school tomorrow painting sets," Gemma said, stretching the dough out in her hands.

"Welcome home," Claire smiled and gave him a kiss on the cheek before grabbing another slice of pepperoni and popping it into her mouth. She headed back to the living room to unload her bags, but not before he swiped her bottom with a dish towel. She smiled back at him.

As she walked out of the room she could feel the weight of the week rolling off her shoulders. She decided to leave her work bags for later. She went upstairs instead to take a shower and wash the day off. Knowing that Patrick was home, the kids were being cared for and she didn't have to make dinner had lightened her mood. She was looking forward to a nice weekend.

SEVEN

Becca woke up Saturday morning feeling sick to her stomach. Sunday was the monthly family dinner, and she absolutely hated these dinners. They were having the dinner on a different weekend to fit in between Thanksgiving and Christmas. She didn't even know why they needed to have dinner together since they would see each other on both holidays. She'd much rather have been with her horses. She threw the white down comforter over her head in dramatic fashion. She had no desire to get out of her warm, comfy bed. On top of not wanting to get out of her comfortable bed, it was her turn to host the family dinner which meant she had to get up so she could clean her house and go grocery shopping. She was not looking forward to the day.

Whenever she was with her family, she always felt like she had to put on a mask. The I'm a successful, independent, single female lawyer don't judge me mask. But she always felt judged. As the oldest of the Flannigan sisters, it was her job to be the example for her sisters as her parents always said. *You're the big sister, you need to show the little girls what to do.* This was the difference between Becca and her two younger sisters. She was the oldest and they were the two little girls. Even though she was closer in age to Elana than Elana and Claire were. All three girls shared a special bond and a bedroom growing up, but when Becca got her period, their mother decided it was time she had a room of her own, so the little girls didn't have to learn about all of that. Her mother didn't celebrate her for becoming a woman as her friend's moms did for them. Getting her period felt like a punishment. Her sisters did still climb into her bed at night or came to her when they needed mothering, but it wasn't the same as all of them being together in the same room. While Becca was in the bedroom next door, she could hear the two little girls chatting and giggling at night while she was all by herself, alone.

That's exactly how Becca always felt, alone. She and Elana were three years apart. Elana and Claire were five years apart. When Claire was born Becca was already in school full-time, Elana part-time. Their mother decided to open a home daycare. Justine took in three other children, and they all played together while Becca was at school all day. When she got home, she was expected to help with the little ones. At the time, she liked it a lot, being the big kid, acting all grown up. But in hindsight she realized she never really had a childhood of her own. She went from an only child to big sister to babysitter. She was a natural caretaker, but her mother had a specific way that caring for the kids needed to be done. Everything was organized and in its place, even people. They all had assigned places to put their shoes, hang their coats, special clothes for school and play and assigned chairs at the dinner table. Becca was responsible for her siblings while her mother looked after the other kids. As soon as Becca walked through the door from school she was on duty.

This mentality that she grew up with followed her into her adulthood. Her two-story townhouse reflected organization. Just enough throw pillows on the couch to make it look homey, not too many to make it crowded. The perfect number of pictures on the wall, balancing art, and family photos. She was proud of her home and of the work she did to be able to afford her home. Everything in order, everything in its place.

The only time she ever felt any freedom was when she was taking care of her horses. Her family knew she owned two horses, but they never asked her about them. There was so much freedom when she rode, so much joy caring for her girls as she referred to them. She loved brushing them, clearing out their shoes and yes, even cleaning their stalls. Rascal and Winnie were her children, she loved them, and they loved her. Her weekends were usually spent at the barn or out in the fields riding. But this weekend, she would have to get her house ready to host the family and spend most of it cooking. She was dreading it. Nine adults and five children in her space—her refuge—was not how she wanted to spend her weekend. She also had a few contracts to go over for work before Monday morning. She threw the sheets over her head as if to block out any more thoughts of what needed to be done like they were the boogie man trying to get her.

After a few more grumbles under the white sheets, Becca dragged herself out of bed and to her dresser. She got dressed in her cleaning clothes. Of course, she had specific clothes for cleaning. Then she headed to the laundry room to gather up the cleaning supplies.

It took her two hours to clean the townhouse. She could have done more, but she knew with all the kids in the house, it was just going to be destroyed anyway. She loved being an aunt, she just wished she had more of a relationship with Claire's kids. She wished she were the "fun aunt," but that title went to Elana. Even though she was three hours away, Elana still got to be the fun aunt by showing up with gifts from The Treasure Trove. She would take the kids outside and chase them around or tell them funny stories about the customers who came into her shop. Becca felt like she just couldn't win with her family, even with the next generation. Being a real estate lawyer wasn't the most exciting job to a child. She didn't think they would want to hear about the closing on a house or a contract that fell through last minute.

After a shower, a well-deserved cup of coffee and a late breakfast, it was time to hit the grocery store for all the ingredients for Sunday dinner. Whoever hosted made enough for everyone. That was all fine and good for the other members of the families, but she was one person and there were between two to five members of all the rest of them. They thought because she was a lawyer with no children she had money oozing out of her pockets. Maintaining her townhouse, barn fees, and caring for the horses was expensive and a portion of her work was pro bono. She liked it that way. Being a real estate lawyer, she was able to do pro bono work helping low-income families fight their dirty landlords. It was work she was proud of. She liked being able to give back to families in the community who couldn't afford the cost of a lawyer. She couldn't believe how many landlords took advantage of their tenants because they knew they didn't have the money to fight back. This desire to help those less fortunate stemmed from growing up and taking care of her siblings and the other children in her mother's care. In a way it filled that void for her. No one in her family knew about her pro bono work. It was another part of life she kept to herself, like her horses.

Becca was turning the key in her front door, as her cell phone began to ring. With reusable bags on her arms and her purse strap sliding off her shoulder, she reached around to the front pocket of her purse to locate her phone. "Hel...hello," she said, trying to balance the phone on her shoulder while kicking the door closed with the back of her heel.

"Becca, it's Mom. Listen tomorrow I'm going to come a little early to help you get ready. You shouldn't have to do it all yourself, and I'll bring something for dessert. Okay, was there anything else?"

"No, I don't think so. But you don't have to. I just got back from the store and bought stuff to make dessert." Becca almost dropped the phone while trying to put the grocery bags on the counter.

"Don't bother, I got it. I'll see you tomorrow. Okay? Did you need anything else?"

"No, I'm good."

"Good." And her mother hung up. That was how every phone conversation with her mother went. She would call someone, never say hello, or ask how they were, and then act like the person had called her and then want to know what they wanted. One day, she'd love her mom to just call to say hello and ask how she was doing, but that was never the case. It was consistently a demand, an order, or a direction.

Becca finally got all her grocery bags on the counter and started unpacking them. "Time to prepare for tomorrow." She began taking out various pots and pans. "Alexa play Stevie Wonder mix," she said to the Echo on her counter.

"Stevie Wonder playlist playing from Spotify," Alexa responded. Becca took her apron off the back door of her pantry and got into her cooking groove with some fun background music.

***

JUSTINE AND JOE ARRIVED FORTY-FIVE MINUTES BEFORE EVERYone else. Her mom briefly knocked and walked in. "Hello, anybody home," she yelled as she came through the door with a plastic wrapped tray in her hands.

Who else would be here?

"Oh good, you're here. Joe, put that stuff on the kitchen counter and then go watch television," she commanded. The dutiful husband did what he was told. "Listen, Becca. I know you have this all under control. I'll just help set the table or whatever else I can do."

Justine got crazy when it was her family's turn to host. She did not want to deal with Patrick's mother's judgmental words and little comments she liked to drop. Becca rolled her eyes. She knew she needed to give her mother a task to keep her busy and out of her hair. "If you could set the table, that would be great. I'm going to finish prepping the salad, which means we will need salad bowls."

"Got it, on it," her mom said as she got busy fussing around the dining room with placemats, cloth napkins, and utensils ordered perfectly. Becca closed her eyes and took a deep breath. She had a feeling she would be doing that a lot throughout the afternoon. By one o'clock, her house was filled with people and noise. The younger kids were running around, and the older kids were sitting on the couches with their faces staring at their cell phones. Occasionally, they would show videos to each other. So much for quality family time. Greg and Joss were discussing or arguing over something to do with the new babies and car seats. The two grandfathers were wrapped up in whatever sport was on television. Margie was sharing gossip to Justine about all of the women in her social group. Becca was standing at the kitchen island taking it all in. She looked over at Claire and Patrick, who were sitting at the dining room table surrounded by the remaining dishes from dinner. *They have been so quiet today; they look exhausted.*

"Claire, Patrick, how is the new schedule working out for you guys," Becca asked across both rooms. "How's the new job, Patrick?" Becca could visibly see Patrick cringe when she asked him the question. She and Patrick had repeatedly butted heads over the years. They didn't agree on social issues, family issues, or political issues. Whenever they tried to have a civilized conversation with each other, it would always end up in a disagreement over something. No matter what her intent for the question was, he was going to take it the wrong way.

"We're managing," Claire chimed back. Patrick nodded in agreement.

"Well, I don't know how Patrick is doing it all. Flying across the country twice a week, working non-stop in between and then taking care of his family when he's home. It's a wonder he is still standing." Leave it to Margie to completely disregard Claire's part in caring for her family. Becca couldn't stand how Margie belittled Claire. She wished Claire would stand up for herself with her mother-in-law more.

"Mom, it's a team effort. Claire and I *together* are making it work," he said in Claire's defense.

"Oh, I'm sure she's doing her best," she said sardonically. Claire was looking at Becca instead of her mother-in-law. She felt flames shooting out of her ears and turned her head to glare at Margie. Becca made eye contact with Margie and opened her mouth slightly ready to say something. Instead, she closed her eyes and took a deep breath.

"Has Grayson started soccer yet?" Joss chimed in, changing the subject.

"Yeah, orientation was yesterday. This week will begin the full schedule," Claire replied.

"Wow, isn't that going to be a lot to manage with Gemma's theater, your work, and picking up Brita from daycare?" Joss asked Claire. Becca thought she was trying to point out to Margie how much Claire was doing. Unfortunately, it fell on deaf ears.

"Yes, we'll figure it out. Carpooling should help," she said in response. Becca saw Patrick grab Claire's hand that was sitting on the table and give it a gentle squeeze. Regardless of how she and Patrick felt about each other, she could see how much he loved her sister.

She watched as Claire made eye contact with him and then asked, "If anyone is available to help out with transporting the kids a couple of days this week, we'd love the extra set of hands, especially if there is an emergency."

"Well, dear, as Becca said when we were together last time. You can't expect us all to just drop our lives and our own schedules for choices you both made," Margie started. Becca shook her head slightly and turned away from the conversation. She knew she did not say that when they were together at Thanksgiving. *Margie* was the one who said it. Becca did not like how Margie was throwing everyone else under the bus.

"We are not asking that at all, Mom. What Claire means is if anyone had some availability, and they want to spend extra one-on-one time with their grandchildren they could go to theater rehearsal or soccer practice or pick up Brita from daycare." *Wow, impressive Patrick, bravo for turning it around.* Becca was impressed.

"Well, of course, we want to spend time with our grandchildren, don't we, Justine," Margie said looking at Claire's mother, who nodded without saying anything. "I'll just have to check our calendar when I get home and get back to you." Margie did not like to commit to anything that would take her away from her social events. They all knew this.

"Claire, I'll find out from our handyman what days he's planning to come and re-paint the rooms that need to be done before listing. You know we will do what we can for you all," her father spoke up. "Becca, how about you?" he asked her sister.

"Oh, don't be ridiculous, Joe. Becca is a career woman; she's too busy to run kids to soccer practice," Margie dismissed Joe's offering with a wave of her hand. By kids she meant Claire's son, her grandson.

Becca looked extremely uncomfortable being put on the spot. "Um...of course I'll do what I can. I'll call you, Claire, and we can discuss." *We can discuss. That sounded so formal. Why didn't I didn't I just say yes. Why is it so hard for me to have a normal conversation with these people?* Becca felt her heartbeat faster in frustration with herself. When they were younger, she would have jumped right in and not only offered to help but would hold the others accountable to do their part as well.

Becca saw George slowly stand up from the couch and fix his pant legs. That was the cue that the dinner gathering was coming to an end. "Welp looks like it's time for us to be heading out. Seventh inning stretch and all." *Were they even watching baseball?*

Everyone started to gather their belongings and children and began to say their goodbyes. Becca patted Claire on the arm. "I'll call you," she said, and Claire mumbled something in reply she did not hear.

She watched Claire hug her mother-in-law who said, "I'll call you; we'll discuss schedules." Another mumble from her. This continued around each adult family member. Their father was dawdling, he seemed to be waiting to be the last to say his goodbye.

He stepped up to Claire. He held her by her shoulders and looked her into her eyes. "Claire bear, I'm here for you. Send me Grayson's soccer schedule. I'll take care of transporting him. Take it off your to-do list. I got it." Becca was grateful for her father in that moment.

"Oh, my goodness, Dad. Do you mean it?" Claire asked, staring back at him in shock.

"Of course. I'm retired. What else do I have to do with my time? Besides, I get to watch my grandson play soccer which is a treat for me. I never got to do that when you girls were little." He was right, he worked so much while they were growing up, he rarely made it to any of the girls' activities. Becca was happy he could do this for Claire. Becca knew she should offer to help as well. She would have to check her work schedule first to see if she had any time available.

EIGHT

On the drive home, Claire filled Patrick in on the conversation with her father. "That was really nice of him to offer," he said.

"That's exactly what I thought." She playfully backhanded his shoulder as he drove them back home for Sunday night prep.

"Ow..." He laughed and rubbed his shoulder. "Now if we could get the rest of our family to chip in, that would be fantastic. Like your sister. I don't understand why she doesn't offer to spend time with her nieces and nephew. At least, Greg and Joss have the kids over for playdates now and then."

"Patrick, I don't want to get into it with you. Becca has a really busy career. She works long hours and doesn't have the time." Claire knew she was making excuses for her sister. She assumed she worked long days like their father did, but she honestly had no idea what Becca did with her time.

"Aunt Becca's a grumpy bird," Brita chimed in from the backseat. Patrick chuckled.

"She's not a grumpy bird," Gemma replied, "She's just misunderstood."

Wow, where did that come from? I didn't even know Gemma was paying attention to our conversation with her head so deep in her phone.

"I just wish Elana lived closer." Claire missed her sister being closer even though it had been over a decade since she had moved to the Cape. Elana was always good about keeping in touch with her and Becca after they moved out of their parents' house. Even if it were just a text message, she would do a weekly check in with them. Claire and Becca lost their connection after Becca left for college. Their relationship has never been the same.

"Me too," said Brita. "I love Aunt Laney. She's fun. She gives me piggyback rides and throws me on the couch, and we play Play-Doh and go to the playground, and she brings me presents and, and everything."

Claire laughed. "I wish I could be the fun one too," she said to no one in particular. *Instead, I get to be the purpose person all the time. I cook the meals, do the laundry, clean the house, there's no fun in that.*

After they arrived home and got the kids bathed and settled in for the night, Patrick and Claire finally got to sit quietly together on the couch for the first time that day. She snuggled up next to him and curled her legs underneath her. She had her fingers curled around a cup of chamomile tea. He wrapped his arm around her and reached for the remote. "Wait," she said and stopped his hand. "Can't we talk for a few minutes."

"Sure, what do you want to talk about?" He put the remote control back down on the coffee table.

"Um..." She contemplated. They've talked about the kids, schedules, family stuff, and what else. "I paid all of our bills last Sunday night." She took a sip of her tea, proud of herself and them.

"That's what we were going to talk about, paying bills?"

"No, Patrick, listen. I paid *all* our bills last Sunday night."

"Every one of them for the month?"

"Every one of them." She blew on her tea and took another sip.

"Wow, that's a reason for a celebration," he said laughing and leaned over to kiss her. She laughed too, realizing she couldn't remember when she last laughed or when they last laughed together. He gently pulled away. "I know this can't be easy for you, Claire. I'm sorry." He brushed a whisp of hair away from her eyes, leaned in, and rested his forehead to hers.

"It's okay. We'll manage. I'll manage." she said as they slowly sat up. "I'm not going to lie to you. It's exhausting. It's hard doing it all on my own all week long. I miss our teamwork. I miss you. We juggled it all together. I really don't know how single parents do it. I have so much more respect for them. I wish, with all that we have done for our families, they would offer to help us out. I mean how many times has your mom called and asked you to come over to help your dad with something? Whenever my dad is sick, or his arthritis is bothering him, you go over and mow their lawn without even being asked. How many trips to various stores have I made for both mothers? I feel like an ungrateful brat, but this isn't for us, it's for the kids. I mean I get Greg and Joss. They are in the same situation as us, sort of. But both sets of parents are retired. I don't understand."

"I know," he said, and she saw him deflate. She wanted to tell him to call his parents and talk to them, but she knew he struggled with his relationship with them as well. The boys kept the peace in the family by keeping Margie happy. If Margie had wanted to help, she would have offered. "It's going to get easier. I promise. And your dad taking Grayson to soccer will be a help."

"Yes," she agreed. "A huge help."

NINE

The week went by in a blur. Every morning was still a battle with Gemma. With Patrick not home, she was trying to push the boundaries with the outfits she wore to school which resulted in huge arguments. Claire was ready to pull all of the tops she had outgrown out of her wardrobe so she couldn't turn them into crop tops. She just needed to find the time to do it. In addition, Claire kept forgetting it was her job to not only wake Gemma up, but to make sure she actually got up. Half the time, Claire called her cell phone to get her out of bed because at least she answered her phone. Thankfully, Grayson made sure he and Brita had breakfast each morning otherwise they may not have eaten at all. Claire was all over the morning routine the first few weeks of Patrick's new job and now it all had gone to hell.

Thursday morning, she raced into her classroom while looking down at her shirt to make sure it was not inside out. Greta poked her head around the doorframe. "Good morning, or was it?" she asked, looking at Claire in her disheveled state.

"No, not a good morning. Gemma was on my last nerve. I swear she knows exactly what to say to dig in a little deeper with her verbal sword. I hate starting my day with an argument and I swear, she almost needs it. It's like it gets her revved up for the day. Like she's so proud of herself for knowing she sent me off to school in a bad mood."

"Well, not to add to the stress of the morning, but I wanted to remind you next week is the holiday luncheon for staff, and our team signed up to make cupcakes. Don't worry about it though," Greta said, holding up a hand. "I got you covered. I'm making enough from both of us. Also, our students' choral concert is on Thursday night." Claire could see her physically cower out the door, but before she snuck away then she said, "and our SLOs were due last week."

"Are you freaking kidding me? How the hell did I forget? Oh my gosh, now I know what I'll be doing with my weekend." SLOs were Student Learning Objectives and something all teachers needed to do for accountability on how students were growing throughout the year. Basically, more paperwork for teachers.

SLOs were the thorn in all teacher's side. It wasn't collecting the data itself, even though it was super time consuming. It was the amount of time it took to write them and put them into the computer system. Then they had to meet with the principal to go over them and be observed. It was a lot of extra work teachers didn't need added onto their plates. It was more to make the district look good to the state than for the teachers and students benefit. She finally made her way over to her desk and started unloading her bags. She realized she left her lunch in the car and would have to find time to run out and get it. Today was a day the kids didn't have a special, so she would need to go at lunchtime and get it. Luckily, it was cold enough outside she knew her salad would not wilt in the car. *Who am I kidding? I'll probably eat Hershey kisses for lunch.*

That night, Patrick called after the kids went to bed. Even though she was sad he didn't get to talk to them, she was also glad because their night was crazy between theater club, soccer practice, dinner, Brita deciding it was more fun to eat spaghetti with her hands then her fork, and Claire having to clean up the mess. She also wanted to pick up the house before Patrick got home so it didn't look like a complete disaster. She looked around the living room at the backpacks piled up by the door, her school papers strewn across the coffee table, and Brita's toys spread out on the floor. *This house is a disaster and I'm too tired to care.*

"Hey," he said when she answered. "You sound beat."

"Yeah, it was a day," she said between two yawns.

"I'm sorry."

"You don't have to keep saying that every time you call, you know." Claire put the phone on speaker so she could get into her pajamas.

"I'm sorry." She could hear the anguish in his voice.

"Patrick." She wanted to say something to ease his mind, but she was too tired to think of anything.

"Sorry, I mean, I wish I could be there to help."

"I know." She moved the clothes she wore that day on the floor from her bed and crawled under the covers.

"I'll be there tomorrow night."

"I have some bad news though. My SLOs were due last week, and I completely forgot about them. I need to finish them up this weekend. Also, next week is the holiday choral concert for my class and I have to be at school Thursday night." Claire bit the inside of her cheek.

"Okay, so what does that mean exactly?" he asked.

"It means I need someone to pick Brita up from daycare, Gemma up after play practice, and then watch the kids until I get home. Oh, and feed all three dinner as well." She dropped her voice to a quiet whisper. "Do you think you could come home early next week?"

"Oh babe, I don't know."

"Can you ask?" She was trying hard not to get upset. This was one of the moments where she knew she needed to ask for help. She's not good at asking for help, she's used to fending for herself. Patrick had been the exception. There was something about the distance that was making asking him for help feel uncomfortable to her.

"I'll try, but I really doubt it as the plane ticket is already booked and we have set schedules for what needs to get done." She could hear the guilt in his voice.

"It's fine. I'll figure it out." Claire pulled the covers closer to her neck.

She wished she could submerge herself underneath all of the blankets and sheets and not come out until Patrick's project was over. A thickness in her throat signaled the onset of tears coming.

"No, don't say that. *We'll* figure it out." They hung up soon after as neither one of them had much to say and they were both too tired for small talk.

***

CLAIRE SPENT THE WEEKEND DIVIDING HER TIME BETWEEN writing her SLOs for work, driving Gemma to and from her social activities and attending Grayson's soccer games. Luckily, Greg and Joss were able to take Brita for a few hours, so Brita didn't have to be stuck in the car while they did all their weekend stuff. Unlike when she was a kid herself. She shook her head to take away the memories of sitting in the back of her mom's old Toyota Corolla while her sisters jumped in or out of the car from wherever they had been.

By Sunday night, she had magically finished all the prep for the week and her work obligations. Claire and Patrick were able to tackle the household chores and spend time with the kids, but unfortunately, not each other. They were more like tag team wrestling partners high fiving each other in and out of the ring.

She was sitting up in bed watching him repack his suitcase for the week ahead. "Is it getting old yet?" she asked.

"What?" he looked up from his suitcase at her.

"Traveling back and forth, packing and unpacking?" She leaned over and helped him fold a shirt.

"Not yet. I'm sure it will though. I was thinking of keeping a set of clothes and essentials there, so I won't have to keep bringing a suitcase. I'm trying to travel more efficiently."

Claire felt a lump in her throat as she thought about him having another life somewhere outside of their family. It was one thing for him to travel back and forth, but to have things permanently at the corporate apartment made it feel so separate, so permanent. She drew her knees up into her chest deciding not to say anything as she didn't want to end their visit in a fight. *Visit? Is this where we are at now? He visits their home?* She decided to change the subject.

"So, what do you have going on this week?" She picked up his socks and started to roll them in a tight ball.

"The usual, the desks should be going in soon, then the computers and then we can start to do the install." Claire swore he spoke a foreign language when he talked about his job. "How about you?" he asked.

"I have a choral concert this week, remember?" They looked at each other and their eyes grew large.

"The kids," they said in unison.

"Don't worry," he said. "I've got it covered." He raced out of the room grabbing his cell phone off the dresser before heading out the door. Ten minutes later he walked back in the room. Claire had changed into her pajamas and was reading a book in bed. "All set," he said.

"All set? Meaning what?" she asked, placing the book faceup on her lap.

"My dad will pick Brita up from daycare, drop her off here where my mom will watch the kids. Then he will get Gemma from play practice. Your dad has Grayson's soccer covered. So, we're good." He looked so proud of himself. It was rather endearing.

"We're good," she said giving him a smile. *Okay, tag teaming with the grandparents.* "This will be fine. It will be fine." Was she saying it to convince him or herself?

***

THURSDAY WAS A LONG DAY. THEY HAD AN ASSEMBLY IN THE MORNing for the kids to sing in front of the whole school. The teachers were expected to teach lessons afterwards to students who were all abuzz with the excitement for the upcoming holiday break. After the kids left, Claire decided to go on Amazon and try to get some Christmas shopping done.

She felt the start of a headache coming on from all that still needed to be done for Christmas or maybe because she knew her in-laws would be taking care of the kids and she feared she was not fully prepared for it.

She tried to clean up the house the night before by making up neat piles from all the messes around the house. The morning didn't help though. She and Gemma were knocking heads again. She didn't get a chance to load the dishwasher after breakfast as she needed to get Brita to daycare and herself to work on time.

Okay, I'm spiraling now. Deep breaths, Claire. She turned back to her computer and the open Amazon webpage. She began to search for the items on Grayson's Christmas list. She was trying to order as much online as possible to make holiday shopping easier. Her plan was to have all the gifts delivered to her parents' house and wrap them all there.

After a fun, loud, and successful holiday concert where she felt like she talked to every parent of current and former students, Claire opened her car door and put her school bags on the passenger seat. Her head was pounding with a full-blown migraine. She turned the key in the ignition, closed her eyes and took a moment to herself. She was not ready to face going home to her in-laws, the state of her house, and the kids. She wished she could crawl through her bedroom window, into her bed and under the covers without anyone seeing her.

The seatbelt light was flashing and beeping which wasn't helping the pounding behind her right eye. She put her seatbelt on to make it stop, but it kept beeping. The sound was beeping at the same rhythm as the pounding in her head. *Please, make it stop*. She looked at the dashboard and saw the signal was for the passenger seat. Her school bags were too heavy, and the car thought it was another passenger. Shaking her head, she moved the bags from the seat to the floor and put the car in reverse.

She was so tired she barely remembered the drive home. At this point in the day, she was running on autopilot. As she walked in the front door, she found her in-laws sitting side-by-side on the couch with their arms folded across their chests. Her father was in the old leather chair looking extremely uncomfortable.

"Everything okay," she said, dropping her bags by the front door.

"Well, Claire, we are all a little worried about you. We thought you were doing fine with Patrick gone, but coming here tonight, we can see you are in over your head." Margie waved her hand around the room with emphasis. Claire looked around. Her house looked lived in. Sure, there were all the piles of stuff neatly stacked about, but it's not as bad as it could be.

"I did not have time to do the dishes this morning and we grocery shop and do laundry on the weekends," she said quietly and a bit under her breath while picking at her cuticles.

"Yes, but there was nothing for dinner for the kids to eat." Margie said, as to push her point across further.

"Thursdays are breakfast for dinner night, we usually have pancakes and eggs. The kids know this." Claire realized she was throwing her kids under the bus now.

"Maybe so, but there was not enough for everyone. Gramps ran and picked up take-out Chinese, which of course we don't mind doing." Margie turned to look at George placing a sympathetic hand on his crossed arms as if he were a saint for feeding his grandchildren.

Claire's heart fell deeper into her chest. She was feeling attacked. She looked to her dad, who was still sitting quietly, for help. Her father ran his hands up and down his pant legs before speaking. "Margie, I'm sure Claire and the kids have it all under control. I've been driving Grayson back and forth to soccer for a few weeks now and everything seems like it's running like fine, oiled machinery." Claire smiled a little at her father. At least she felt he was in her corner even if he was being awkwardly put in the middle of Claire and her in-laws.

Margie ignored Joe and continued her rant. "I also gave Brita a bath tonight and she dumped a whole bottle of baby powder on her head. It was a huge mess and I had to start all over again."

"She's Grandma," Claire said with a smirk. Pride covered her face, and she saw her dad trying not to laugh.

"What does that mean?" Margie said with annoyance.

"When her preschool celebrated their 100th day of school last year she dressed up like a one-hundred-year-old grandma. We put baby powder in her hair to make it white. She thought it was hysterical and since then, she occasionally likes to see herself look like grandma again."

"Well, whatever the case may be, it was a complete mess." Margie was staring at her in utter exasperation. She got up from the couch. "Come on, George. It's time to go. Claire, when Patrick gets home you might want to reevaluate how this new situation is working out for you." Margie and George put on their coats and headed to the door.

"Thank you for watching the kids tonight," Claire said, looking forward to closing the door behind them. She walked over to the couch and fell in complete exhaustion. "Well, that sucked."

"Claire bear, take her with a grain of salt. Nothing will ever be right unless it's done her way. Then it won't be right unless she's the one to do it. You're doing fine." Claire glanced over at her father from her spot on the couch. He may have not been the most involved father growing up, but he was an extremely sweet man.

"Thanks, Dad, it really means so much," tears formed in her eyes. Her father slowly rose from the chair, his knees cracking in the process.

"You're going to be okay, kiddo." Claire half smiled up at him and he bent down and kissed her on the top of her head. Claire shut her eyes and heard the door close as he left.

***

CHRISTMAS BREAK COULDN'T ARRIVE FAST ENOUGH. PATRICK had only been in his new position for a month, but it felt like a year. She and Patrick were so excited to have a week at home with the kids. They were hosting Christmas Eve dinner this year. Elana was driving into town with Danny, and she was so excited to see her sister.

"Claire bear," Elana said, running into the kitchen arms spread wide for a hug. She stopped short. "Oh my god, you look like hell."

"Really, Laney!" Becca said from the kitchen counter, where she was creating a veggie platter in the shape of a Christmas tree.

"I'm sorry, but she does." Elana put the bags hanging off her arms down on the floor. Claire wiped her hands on her apron and opened the refrigerator door to hide her face as her eyes filled with tears. She needed to control this crying impulse she was developing. She needed a better poker face.

Patrick walked in carrying the appetizer tray Elana brought. "My god, Patrick, what have you done to my sister?" Patrick looked to Elana and then over Claire, who had moved back to the counter, and then back to Elana.

"What?" he looked to Claire with a furrowed brow as if asking her what he was missing.

"Look at her. She's wasting away. She's so thin and she doesn't look like she's slept in months." Claire composed herself. She turned to look at her sisters and husband. "I'm fine, guys, really. It's been a busy few weeks. Between work and getting ready for the holidays, it's just been busy," she said, turning to all three of them with the biggest, fake smile she could muster on her face.

"Oh, you are not fine," Becca stated firmly. "Do you see what you are doing to her?" she said glaring at Patrick.

"What am I doing to her?" he exclaimed as he looked to Claire for some help. She could see in his eyes he was readying himself for an argument with Becca, but it was Christmas Eve and Claire needed to diffuse the situation.

"Stop, I'm fine," she said emphatically.

"Regardless of how you say you are, I hope you take some time this week to rest. You honestly do look drained." Claire knew Elana was coming from a place of love, but her words were super hurtful to her. Claire had vented to Elana how tired she was on Friday. She didn't need her sister now verbalizing it to Patrick and Becca.

"Okay, okay. I got it. I look tired. Now the three of you get out of my kitchen. You're ruining my Christmas cheer. I am trying to deck the freaking halls here." She let out a fake laugh and then shooed them all out of the room with the wave of her hand. She could hear the three of them bickering amongst themselves as they walked into the living room. This was a day she wished her house were bigger so she could separate herself more from the conversation she was overhearing. Her sisters were laying into her husband about him stepping up more when he was home or getting her more help when he was not. Neither one of them had any idea how hard she and Patrick were *both* trying to make this work.

Claire enjoyed Christmas day so much more than Christmas Eve. Christmas morning was customarily spent with her, Patrick, and the kids. They opened presents, ate leftovers throughout the day, snuggled in their pajamas, and watched Christmas movies. Patrick's parents went to Joss' house with her family. Elana spent the morning with her ex-husband and son as his family lived close by. Then Elana headed to their parents' house to have dinner with Becca and their parents while Danny stayed with Mark. It was the only holiday she got to have her immediate family to herself. It was her favorite day of the year. The last thing she needed was her two sisters getting in an argument with her husband, him getting into a bad mood and risk ruining her favorite day.

Twenty minutes later she walked into the living room. There was sports on the television, the kids were playing a board game, and the adults were talking amongst themselves. Things seemed to have settled down. Claire could breathe easily. "Dinner will be ready in five. I could use some help carrying the dishes to the buffet table." Claire walked back into the kitchen looking forward to the other side of the day when she and Patrick could read the kids *'Twas the Night Before Christmas* and tuck them into bed. Then they got to play Santa Claus before crawling into bed themselves. Patrick's favorite part was getting to eat half of the cookies and drink some of the milk. Another thing Claire found so lovable about him; he embraced family traditions.

TEN

Becca hated Christmas. It was a reminder she was alone. No family of her own, no children to have Christmas morning with. Everyone thought she had chosen to be unmarried and childless. It wasn't true. She didn't correct them either. She couldn't say how she truly felt. She wished she had what Elana and Claire have. A family of her own. Yes, Elana and Mark were divorced, but they did an amazing job of co-parenting Danny. They spent all the important moments as a threesome and still took a family vacation together once a year. Becca had a few serious relationships over the years, but none of the guys in her life felt like her soulmate. She dated one guy, Leo, who she thought she really loved but he complained that she was emotionally distant and had too many walls up to get close to her. He eventually broke up with her and moved on to someone else, got married, and started a family. She tried not to think about what could have been with him.

Her cell phone pinged with a message. She had poured her first cup of coffee. She turned her phone over and saw a message from Elana.

Merry Christmas

Same to you

You okay?

Meh

Do you want me to come over?

It's okay. I'm going to see Rascal and Winnie

K. Have fun. See you tonight

See you tonight

Becca appreciated Elana consistently checking in on her. They didn't talk often, but Elana somehow always knew the exact moment Becca needed to hear from her. She got herself dressed in her horse-riding gear. She was looking forward to spending a quiet morning at the barn with her horses. Being with them gave her so much joy. A nice ride on a cold winter's morning would lift her spirits. She walked out into her living room and looked around at the perfectly placed furniture, pillows, and pictures. She needed a little chaos in her life. She didn't know how to get it, but she knew it was time to start living more. She was forty-four and tired of watching others living the life she wanted for herself. She made a Christmas promise to herself this would be the last Christmas she woke up alone.

ELEVEN

Christmas break was exactly what Claire needed. Time with her family, time to recharge. She was looking forward to lazy days in pajamas watching Christmas movies. Time to reconnect with Patrick. A beautiful end to December, but instead they all ended up with the flu. It began the day after Christmas, Brita said she wasn't feeling well after dinner. Claire assumed it was because she ate too much heavy food over the holiday. That was until Brita woke up in the middle of the night vomiting and running a fever.

While Claire cleaned her up in the bathroom, Patrick changed her sheets and blankets and put the soiled ones in the wash. He then put a trash can next to Brita's bed. Claire spent the rest of the night crunched up next to Brita in her toddler bed. Neither one of them slept much as Brita continued to get sick through the night. The next day it hit Grayson. Two days later, all five of them were sick and miserable. Claire did get her lazy days in pajamas, watching movies. Unfortunately, it wasn't the way she was hoping it would be. Between washing sheets, sanitizing the house, and getting sick herself, it was a miserable few days.

By New Year's Eve, everyone was finally feeling better. There was a snowfall which brought six inches of fresh snow. The perfect amount for their small New England town. They met a bunch of families at the hill at the high school during the day. The kids went sledding while the parents hung out and chatted at the top of the hill with coffees. Brita was in heaven with all the attention she was getting from Gemma's friends. New Year's Eve night was quiet. They ordered Japanese food to be delivered and watched Disney movies with Brita. Gemma was at a sleepover. Grayson and Kyle stayed upstairs in his room playing video games with a couple of other friends. The atmosphere emoted cozy. Finally, it was exactly how Claire wanted it.

She fell asleep in bed with Brita around ten p.m. Patrick came upstairs to wake her so they could watch the ball drop together. She was the happiest when she was snuggled on the couch next to her husband. She went to bed that night wishing the happy feeling in her heart would never end.

However, reality hit the following Monday morning. She woke to find Patrick had already left for the airport. She moaned as she rolled over to his empty side of the bed. She pulled his pillow into her, inhaling and taking in his scent. *Eleven more months*. She had a sick feeling in her stomach thinking about having to go back to the hectic weekly routine. After she took a few extra minutes to be lazy, she dragged herself out of bed.

TWELVE

Becca woke up in her oversized bed with a pillow over her face. She had too much to drink the night before and was rocking a horrible hangover. She had met a few lawyer friends at a restaurant in West Harford for a later dinner which led to drinks at the bard afterwards. They lost count on how many bottles of wine they had ordered. She remembered the Uber dropping her off and walking through her front door. She did not remember much after that. Having that many drinks was extremely out of character for her. She was paying for it now as her head throbbed. She knew she needed to get out up and take some Advil, but her pounding head did not want her to move. She pulled her phone off her bedside table to look at the time. 10:15. She hadn't slept that late since her college days. She noticed a message from Elana.

Happy New Year!

Happy New Year.

She typed back with one eye open and the other closed. Three dots appeared and then a message came through.

Patrick left today

I know

She's going to need help

I know

Will you call her later?

I'll try

Becs

I will

Rip the band-aid off

Okay

TTYL

Elana probably knew Becca wasn't going to call Claire. Ever since Becca moved back home after law school, her relationship with Claire had been strained. Becca didn't do a good job of staying in touch with her sisters once she left for college, which was strange considering she was the mother figure to Elana and Claire for so long.

By her senior year, she had had enough of the demands from her mother. She started to pull away from the family, including her sisters. She and Justine were arguing all time because Becca wanted to be out with her friends or doing her own thing and her mother still wanted her to be the surrogate parent to the younger girls, especially Claire. Becca still remembers one of their biggest fights like it had happened yesterday. It happened towards the beginning of the school year, Elana was a freshman and Claire was nine years old.

Their mother had given up her home daycare a few years earlier, once Claire was settled into school full-time. She now helped their father in his law firm a few days a week with bookkeeping. They were in the kitchen, and she was getting ready to leave to meet some friends. Her mother had told, not asked, her to pick up Claire from Girl Scouts.

"Why do I need to pick up Claire from school? She's old enough to take the bus." Becca reached over to the key hook to grab the keys to the used car that her father had helped her buy the summer before.

"Because she had Girl Scouts after school and you're going out anyway." Justine began to take out pots and pans from under the cabinet.

"Yeah, I'm going out with my friends. I don't know when I'll be home, and her school isn't even on the way," Becca said trying to control her tone.

"Well, I've been out all day at the office with your dad and am not planning on going out again. So, go get your sister." Justine continued with her dinner preparations. Becca glanced at the clock. It read four o'clock. She didn't need to make dinner now.

"Are you kidding me? This is ridiculous. You're her mother." Heat flushed through her body; her nostrils flared.

"Well, it's not like I planned to be." Becca couldn't believe she was verbalizing again that Claire was an unplanned pregnancy.

"Oh my god, did you just say that to me? What is wrong with you?" They were standing across from each other. She could feel the anger and heat coming off of herself. She had never been this angry with her mother before, never mind talking to her mother that way.

"I meant she wasn't planned. Claire was an oops, a good oops, but an oops." Her mother was trying to backpedal from what had slipped out of her mouth, but it was too late.

"I can't believe you even said it out loud. It's one thing to think it, Mom, but to say it out loud to me? Elana and I practically raised Claire. What are you going to do next year when I'm at college?" Both of Becca's hands were now on her hips as she glared at her mother.

"You know what, Becca, forget it. I'll get her," Justine said in exasperation.

"No, don't bother. I'll get her. You have until next August, and once I leave, you better figure out how to be a mother." Becca walked out the kitchen door, slamming it behind her.

There was something in the way she spoke to her own mother that shocked Becca. Then it finally clicked for her. Becca didn't want to be part of her mother's "team" anymore. She wanted to be a sister not a mother. She wanted to be a kid, not an adult. Her sisters were old enough to take care of themselves. It was after this conversation Becca began to rebel against their mother. What she didn't realize in doing this was she began neglecting her younger sisters to spite her mother. The ripple effect of that argument began the wedge put between she and Claire. So much time had passed since that day, Becca didn't know how to go about reclaiming the bond they once shared.

THIRTEEN

January and February were a complete fog for Claire. The days were long and tiring. She felt like she was floating around in a daze. She was managing to keep the kids' days as normal as possible. Carpooling with Gemma's friend's families helped, and her father driving Grayson to his indoor soccer practice was also a huge help. It was keeping up with everyday life. The house was falling apart, laundry was piling up as winter was here and there were so many more clothes to wash. Claire couldn't remember the last time she did anything which resembled fun with her family. She wanted to do something about it, but she was always so tired. Greta offered to come over and take the kids out for dinner one night to give her some time to herself, but she was even too tired for that. She felt like she was being buried under her own life.

Claire wondered if she was surviving motherhood or failing at it. It constantly seemed like something was about to crash down on her. She did not read that part in the book, *What to Expect When You're Expecting,* or in *What to Expect the First Years.* Where was the book about *What to Expect for the Rest of their Lives?* The book on how to manage it all when your husband is out of town, and you can barely take care of yourself never mind your children.

And why do schools expect so much from us, she wondered to herself. *Between parties, events, special occasions, and fundraisers it feels like it's never ending. Then it's sign this and bake that and volunteer for this. Then there are the endless project the kids can't do by themselves, and they need our help and then you get frustrated with your child because they're annoying so you have to do it yourself so you can be flipping done and you can get on with spinning your plates.*

Am I surviving motherhood? I really don't know the answer. Claire knew she was spiraling. She also knew she needed to get her frustration out to face the day ahead. She grabbed the blue decorative pillow sitting next to her and screamed into it. She actually felt a little bit better.

Sunday dinner was at their house that week, the worst weekend ever for them to be hosting. Claire spent the morning working on her lesson plans for the week and preparing report cards. She was doing her best to get through all of her schoolwork, so she didn't go into the week already behind.

After a quick lunch from bites of a cheese stick and some crackers thrown into her mouth, she ran around the house with a laundry basket picking up everything on the floor and tossing it into the basket. Once filled, she hid the basket in the laundry closet and then proceeded to fluff throw pillows and fold decorative blankets.

Patrick was outside with Brita getting the grill ready. She had no time to prepare a fancy meal, so he was grilling up chicken and steak. Thankfully, it was an unseasonably warm day out. Claire ran into the kitchen, washed the dishes from breakfast, and wiped down the counters. It would have to do.

Did I shower today? I don't think I showered. She glanced in the hall mirror. She definitely did not shower. She yelled out to Patrick to let him know she was taking a quick shower. He waved his BBQ tongs at her. *Nothing like a man and his grill.*

She raced up the stairs, ran into their bathroom and closed the door. She was completely out of breath. *Maybe it's time to start exercising again.* She took the fastest body shower she'd ever taken, no time for hair today. It's what hair clips were invented for. She threw on whatever was decent and clean. Although, she thought she wore this shirt at their last family dinner. *Crap. Whatever, I don't have time.*

Sitting on the edge of her unmade bed, she closed her eyes and took a deep breath giving herself a little pep talk. *You got this, Claire.* Heading down the stairs, she heard voices in the kitchen. As she walked in, she found her mother and mother-in-law unpacking bags. "Happy Sunday, what do you have there?" she said to them both.

"Oh, Justine and I texted about bringing a few extra things for dinner. We know how busy you all are." Margie pulled out two apple pies and vanilla ice cream from her bag. Justine took out a homemade pasta salad.

Claire turned toward the refrigerator so she could roll her eyes. She did forget about dessert and bought pasta salad from the grocery store. "That was so thoughtful of you both. Thank you," she said as she opened the refrigerator door and quickly moved the store made salad to the back of the shelf. She pulled out a few items from the refrigerator and place them on the kitchen island. "I'm also making a salad and homemade coleslaw to go with the steaks and chicken."

"Sure, if you call a bag of coleslaw and Marie's Coleslaw dressing homemade," Gemma said as she came into the kitchen and swiped a grape tomato. Claire smacked her hand away and scowled at her.

"Gemma, why don't you take the grandmas into the living room and fill them in on all the exciting things going on in your life. Spill the tea." Gemma rolled her eyes at her and headed out of the kitchen.

"Spill the tea. Gemma don't spill your tea. Do you want tea? I can make you some. Do you even drink tea?" Claire's mother said as she followed Gemma. Her mother-in-law approached her and grabbed the hem of her shirt.

"You really like this shirt don't you, dear. Let me know if you'd ever like to go shopping sometime. We could make it a fun girls day." Then she left the room.

I need a glass of wine. Pronto. Claire turned back to the fridge to grab the bottle of white wine. "Did you remember to get more ketchup or BBQ sauce?"

Claire jumped sky high and almost dropped the bottle. "Holy hell, Grayson. I didn't realize you were there." Turning back to the fridge, she scanned the contents. *Oh no, no no no.* She ran to the pantry and flung open the left door. She pulled open the right door. No ketchup. No BBQ sauce. She grabbed one of the bags off the counter.

"Grayson, I need you to run next door to Kyle's house and ask Janie if I can borrow all of the condiments she has in her kitchen." He rolled his eyes at her. "Right now." She shoved his body out the kitchen door and pushed him toward their neighbor's house.

"Tell her I love her, she's my best friend ever, and I owe her a bottle of wine. Also, I will replace everything."

"Moms are so weird," he said under his breath. *Now I'm definitely having a glass of wine.* She filled her wine glass almost to the top and turned around to find her mother-in-law in the kitchen doorway staring at her with judgmental eyes.

***

Everywhere she went, Claire felt like someone was judging her or giving her advice about how to manage her family during the week. Patrick's new job, her issues with her family, and everyone's unrequested opinions were bringing up childhood trauma for Claire. She felt inadequate. She felt like she was letting someone down all the time. Her mind kept reflecting to times in her childhood when she felt like she was disappointing her family. She was trying so hard to make sure her kids did not feel the way she had growing up. She was trying to keep her family unit intact. Yet, she felt like she was losing complete control of it all. She would get looks of pity. People would ask her how Patrick was doing as if he was in the hospital instead of out of town for work. Dropping off Brita at daycare, the teacher would gently place her hand on Claire's arm and ask, "How are you doing?" with a sad expression on her face. He's in Chicago, not dying, she wanted to say.

Mrs. Pratt, her nosey neighbor from down the street, was walking past her house one day. She made a comment to Claire on how she didn't see Patrick around much anymore then asked her if everything was okay with their marriage. She had to explain how he was traveling for work now. Her neighbor's response was, "Well, be careful dear. Distance doesn't always make the heart grow fonder." *Why do people feel like it's okay to say things like that?* Patrick's schedule was getting unpredictable, and he wasn't able to come home every weekend as they planned. She was running on empty.

Work was also getting busier for Claire. Report cards were due soon, the kids had early dismissal, and Claire had to prepare for parent/teacher conferences. Most parents thought early dismissal days were a treat for teachers. They were so much harder than a regular full day. They must keep the kids engaged and learning while moving the lessons along at a much shorter time limit. The kids' specials were abbreviated. Teachers were constantly watching the clock. Then they had to make sure everyone got to their right dismissal location, whether bus or parent pickup. Buses were usually off schedule on early dismissal days, so they would end up waiting for late buses with students. After the kids were picked up, teachers raced back to their classrooms to shove food in their mouths and get ready for their first conference. Claire tried to keep her conferences to fifteen minutes with a ten-minute gap in between, however, it never worked.

Most parents felt judged by their kid's performance whether they were excelling or falling behind, parents felt it's a reflection on them. There were three types of parents, those who cry because their child was doing so well or not so well and then the defensive parents who used every excuse for their child's behavior. The third type were the ones who blamed the teachers for not doing their job to help their child succeed. These were the parents Claire worked way too hard to win over. That was her teaching flaw. She felt the need to prove herself worthy of their child and the parents' acceptance.

Thursday was her long day, kids in the morning, conferences in the afternoon and evening. She had her stack of files on her reading table in order of conferences for the day. She also liked to have the kids' work displayed on the boards outside her room and in the classroom for the parents to see.

After the kids left, Claire prepared herself for a long day of talking. She had her water on the table in front of her, tea with honey, throat lozenges, granola bars and, of course, chocolate. Her in-laws were taking care of the kids again. After the last time they watched the kids, she was worried about what she may go home to.

She scanned the condition of her house in her mind. Lots of laundry on the laundry room floor. Did she remember to load the dishwasher? She should text the kids to make their beds. Was there enough food in the house for dinner? There small house made messes look so much bigger. *Okay, I'm spiraling now. Deep breath, Claire.* The first set of parents came into the classroom. She looked around the room from her seat to make sure the room looked presentable. *I think I am ready.*

Seven hours later, her head was pounding like her heartbeat had moved behind her right eye. She drove home with the left eye open and her right hand covering her right eye. As she approached her house, she noticed a lot of cars in the driveway. She took inventory. She saw her father-in-law's car, her mother-in-law's car, her dad's car, and her sister, Becca's car. *What was she doing here? Oh no, the kids!*

Claire raced into the driveway, threw the car in park, and ran into the house leaving all her school stuff still in the car. "Are the kids okay?" she said breathlessly as she rushed through the front door.

"The kids are fine," her dad said. "They are all up in their rooms waiting for you to get home."

"Why? Why are you all here? Oh, my goodness, is Patrick okay? Did something happen to Patrick?" She was beside herself with worry, her eyes darted around at everyone. Her hand was covering her heart. She looked over at Becca who was not making eye contact with her.

"No, dear, Patrick is fine," her mother-in-law said.

"I don't understand. Then why are you all here?"

"Maybe you should sit down first." Margie pointed to the accent chair next to her fathers. She and George were sitting on the couch side-by-side. Her sister was standing off to the side behind them. Claire walked over and sat down, with her jacket still on. "We think you need help, dear." Margie scowled at Claire.

"Okay..." she said. "So is this like an intervention of some sort." Claire looked over at her dad. He stared at her and shook his head slightly side to side. His gesture to say he was there for support. She stared at him as if saying with her eyes, *What's going on?*

"No, no...not an intervention. More like an organization." Margie looked over at Becca. Becca was standing behind the couch, a notebook in one hand and pen in the other. *It sure felt like an intervention.*

"What do you mean by an organization?" she asked.

"Becca, why don't you explain," Margie said.

"Um...okay," Becca said looking over at Margie. She was obviously uncomfortable being put on the spot. Becca cleared her throat and began to speak in her lawyer voice. "Claire, based upon Margie and George's observations when walking into the house they noticed it to be a bit disheveled. For example, there were stacks of items spread out through each room, dishes overflowing in the sink, and laundry piled up in front of and on top of the washing machine. They also observed there were sparse amounts of food in the refrigerator and pantry." Becca sounded like she was giving a closing argument to prove Claire as an unfit mother.

Does she actually believe all of this or was she separating herself from it by going into lawyer mode? Claire's eyes begin to water. She was feeling attacked by her family. "I did not have time to do the dishes this morning and we grocery shop and do laundry on the weekends." She wanted to defend herself.

"Yes, but there was nothing for dinner for the kids to eat," Margie said.

"Thursdays are breakfast for dinner night, we always have pancakes and eggs. The kids know this. And I've also told you this before." Her resolve to fight for herself diminished with each word.

"Yes, you've said this before, but there were no eggs in the house. We ordered pizza and salad, and there's leftovers in the fridge for you. Oh, I also threw away your baby powder. Now you won't have to worry about Brita turning herself into grandma." Margie said it with a tone as if to say it was the most generous thing anyone had ever done. "Claire, you obviously can't do this on your own which is why I called Becca and asked her to come over. We have put together a schedule to help you on the days Patrick is gone."

She wanted to scream at them all, *Where were you all when Patrick and I first asked for help?* Claire slowly sat back further into the chair. She felt her head begin to spin. The headache behind her right eye was making her feel nauseous. "What kind of schedule?"

"Becca, go ahead." Margie waved a hand over to Becca to hand the intervention over to her sister.

"Well...Dad will continue to take Grayson to and from soccer. I will pick Gemma up from play rehearsal, no more carpooling with her friends, to keep it simpler. You will pick up Brita from daycare on your way home from work. This will give you the opportunity to come home and make dinner and get settled without having to drag Brita back out to get Gemma later. Instead of doing the grocery pick-up order like you usually do, we suggest having it delivered so it's one less stop to make." Becca read from her yellow legal pad without looking up once at Claire.

"And I will come by on Tuesdays and Thursdays to pick up the house and do some laundry. This way there will be less for Patrick to do when he comes home," Margie said with pride. As if the matter was settled and Claire was not allowed any input on this new situation.

"I can drive Brita too," her father-in-law chimed in.

Claire was full blown crying now. Her head felt like it was about to explode, and her heart was hurting. She felt completely incompetent to take care of her own children. They all looked at her like she was crying because she agreed with all of this. She was losing control of her house, and she didn't have the energy to say anything. She wished Patrick were here.

Margie and George stood up from the couch as if to say it was all settled. "Claire, dear, we all love you and want to support you and the kids. We just didn't realize this would be too much for you to manage," Margie said and gave her a half hug before walking to the door. George patted her shoulder as he walked by her. She heard the front door open and close. She sat there stone-cold not understanding what had happened.

"Claire bear, you've been doing a fantastic job. We want you to know we are here to help you and the kids in any way we can. Let's give this a try for a couple of weeks and see how it goes. If it isn't working for you, we can revisit," her dad said as he stood. He leaned down and kissed the top of her head before heading out the door himself.

Becca and Claire were left in the living room alone. She was still standing behind the couch holding the notebook and pen. "What just happened?" Claire muttered tearfully out loud but to herself.

Becca cleared her throat. "I'm sorry, Claire. Margie called me like this was a true emergency. I don't know how to say no to her. She scares me."

"Really," she hissed, a flash of anger lighting her eyes as she looked up at Becca. "So, you go all into lawyer mode on me. Thanks, Becca. Not that I wasn't already having a super shitty day to begin with, then I get home to my family telling me I'm a bad mom and I'm doing a horrible job caring for my own children."

"Claire, that was not what we said or meant." Becca wasn't doing a good job of reassuring her.

"Well, that's what I heard!" Her voice went from shock to anger. "You couldn't have stood up for me? You couldn't have told her you would talk to me on your own instead of being put in front of the firing squad. You know what, never mind, go. You can leave the list for me, so I know what my duties are now."

Becca didn't say anything more. She walked around the couch, grabbed her purse off the table by the door, and slowly left.

Claire sat with her elbows on her knees and her head in her hands. She heard noise on the stairs and slowly glanced up. Gemma and

Grayson were timidly walking down the stairs. "Wow, Mom." Gemma said. "What was that all about?"

"Well, I guess our family thinks I'm doing a crappy job taking care of you guys." Claire didn't have the energy to hold back for the kids. She was too tired and overwhelmed.

"Mom, you know that's not true," Grayson said as he descended the stairs. He sat on the arm of her chair and placed a hand on her back. Gemma sat on the other side and did the same. It felt good to be comforted by her children, but shouldn't it have been the other way around?

"I don't know, you guys. Am I dropping the ball? Have I been slacking on you?" she looked from one to the other.

"No," they said in unison.

"I think it's hard because we were all used to dad being around," Gemma said.

"We can help out more too," Grayson said, laying a reassuring hand on her shoulder. "We can help with dishes and laundry and even make dinner sometimes." Claire didn't even have to look up to see Gemma shoot him a death stare to know she was doing that exact thing behind her back.

"I appreciate you all so much, I really do. We'll give this a try," she said, waiving over at the notepad sitting on the coffee table. "Maybe it will be okay." The tone of her voice didn't sound convincing. She looked up at both of them. "I love you guys, you know that, right?"

"Of course."

"Yeah," they said at the same time.

"Gemma, are you okay with Aunt Becca picking you up from play practice and bringing you home instead of carpooling with your friends."

"Yeah, Mom. I'm good with it." Claire patted both kids on their knees.

"Okay, so I guess Monday starts this new schedule. Let's head up to bed. I need sleep."

After she said one last goodnight to the kids, she peeked in on Brita.

Brita was sound asleep in her toddler bed. She was face down on her pillow with her little tushy sticking up in the air. Claire felt so guilty she missed her tonight. Her little face always made Claire's days brighter.

This had been the longest day ever. She climbed under the covers and turned the light out. She had never loved her bed more than she did at that very moment. Her cell phone rang. She knew it was probably Patrick. She couldn't answer it. There was too much to unpack with him and she couldn't do it tonight. He'd be home tomorrow, and she'd deal with it all then.

FOURTEEN

Becca took the back roads home. She needed to hide in the dark to get away from the awkwardness that had taken place at Claire's house. How was she called into this situation anyway and why didn't she say anything to support Claire?

When Margie called saying she was worried about Claire and the kids, Becca thought something was seriously wrong. With Patrick taking off on her, of course, things were going to be put off; like dishes and laundry.

She felt like she betrayed her sister, and Claire would think she was siding with Margie. Which was why she went into lawyer mode. Anytime she got together with the family she felt like she must put up a protective barrier for herself. The plight of the eldest sister was that she was expected to lead by example for her sisters and was also expected to nurture them. Doing both was exhausting. She knew they all respected what she did for a living, so it was easier to play that role than to be her true self around them. Whoever that was.

As Becca drove down the dark, narrow streets to her townhouse she thought about what she agreed to do. She would drive Gemma home from play practice each week. That's not so bad. She didn't have much of a relationship with her nieces or nephew, but with Gemma being the oldest, maybe she'll have more to talk about with her.

As she pulled into her single garage spot under her townhouse, her phone lit up with a text. She saw Elana's name flashing. She put the car in park and picked up her cell.

How did it go?

How did you know?

Mom

Ah, good gossip.

It was horrible.

Why didn't I speak up for her?

She looked at me like I was her worst enemy.

She'll be okay. We're going to help her through this.

She'll eventually understand it's coming from a place of love.

It did not feel like there was a lot of love in the room tonight.

So, what was your assignment?

Drive Gemma home from theater rehearsal.

That's good. You and Gemma will get along really well.

That's what I'm hoping for. I would like a relationship with Claire's kids.

I'll talk to her.

Thank you, goodnight.

Night.

Becca put her phone in her purse and got out of her Range Rover. She felt better after texting with Elana. This was going to be a good thing. Maybe she and Claire would be able to repair their relationship. Becca would like to get closer to her nieces and nephew. It'd been hard to get close to them with the wall Claire had put up around her family. Also, she and Patrick had never gotten along. All the conversations they have ever had seemed on edge. Becca's not sure why, other than their different stances on certain issues. She assumed Claire must have said something to him about her leaving for college and abandoning Claire. She can't imagine it was easy being left by herself with their mother. Becca knew she should have called Claire and visited her more.

FIFTEEN

Claire's alarm went off at five-thirty. Her eyes didn't seem to want to open. She blinked a few times, then reached for her cell phone. She turned off the alarm and noticed a voice message. She clicked on the little arrow to playback the message.

"Hey babe, I hate to do this, but I'm not going to make it home this weekend. We have an inspector coming through today and I need to be here when he arrives. Unfortunately, we don't know when it will be. It makes more sense for me to stay here this weekend than fly back and forth for one day. Sorry I'm leaving this on a voice message and sorry I won't be home. Please give the kids a big hug and kiss from me and I'll call you all tomorrow. Love you, bye."

She threw her hand over her forehead. *What is happening to my life?* She opened the message app on her phone and texted Greta and Elana.

I need an emergency session this morning or after school.

SOS...911...HELP!

Her phone immediately pinged back.

Greta

We got you

We'll do a virtual happy hour tonight. I'll FaceTime you both at five.

Let's make it 8:30 so I can put Brita to bed first.

She got two thumbs up back. Thank goodness for them. Claire decided to take a mental health day from work. She texted Greta separately to let her know. She also gave her the information to find where her lesson plans were in her classroom for the substitute. She spent the day cleaning the house and doing laundry. She watched horrible reality television and enjoyed every moment of it.

It took her longer to get Brita to sleep that night. Three bedtime stories later and lots of additional hugs, Brita was finally asleep. Grayson was sleeping at Kyle's next door and Gemma was being dropped off after play practice by their carpool. Her last night of carpool.

I'm good now. Grabbing my wine and crawling into bed.

Five minutes later, a FaceTime call popped up on her phone. She answered it and both Greta and Elana's smiling faces popped up on the screen. "Both of your faces are the best thing I've seen in twenty-four hours," she said to them. Then proceeded to fill them in on the week, last night's conversation and Patrick not coming home this weekend. "I am honestly starting to feel like a single parent you guys."

"Wait, can we go back a minute," Greta said. "Your mother-in-law called the family over for an intervention over some piled up dishes, clothes and other crap in your house."

"Yup," she said, taking a big gulp of her red wine. *Drinking wine in bed. Why have I never thought to do this before?*

"Hell, I'd hate for her to see the condition of my house and it's only me and Ray now."

"What I don't get is why Mom was not there?" Elana chimed in.

"Because she was scared to say anything in front of Margie is what I figure, especially if she disagreed with her. The thought of having my mother-in-law in my house twice a week to clean up and do laundry makes me feel nauseous. And I haven't even had a chance to talk to Patrick about all of this."

"Are you sure he doesn't already know?" Elana asked. "Maybe he asked his parents to help out." That thought had not occurred to her.

"I don't know. Can you all tell me about your lives or anything else? I'm so tired of my own life. Tell me a story or some gossip to take me away." she said, sliding further into her pillows and under her covers with her glass of red wine in hand and a few chocolates waiting to be consumed on the bedside table.

An hour later, Gemma came walking up the stairs. She poked her head into the room and found her mother lying in bed with an empty wine glass and candy wrappers on the bedside table. Claire was half asleep but trying to stay awake to wait for her.

"Rough week?" she asked, nodding her head at the remnants from the night. She sat down on the edge of the bed.

"Yeah. Dad's not going to make it home this weekend." Claire sat up a little to talk to her daughter.

"Yeah, you told us already." Gemma fiddled with a loose thread on the comforter.

"Oh, I did, sorry, I'm extremely tired." Claire glanced over at the clock on the table. It was only nine o'clock, but it felt like midnight to her.

"It's okay, Mom. You can go to sleep." Gemma began to stand up from the bed.

"How was play practice?" Claire said through a yawn.

"It was good, really good. We are in decent shape. The actors are almost all off book, and the sets are painted and starting to be assembled. This is the first play I've ever done that we have been this far ahead of schedule." She could see the excitement in her daughter's eyes as she talked.

"Oh, honey. I am so glad to hear it. I'm so happy for you." Her eyes grew heavier and heavier with each word.

"Goodnight, Mom."

"Night, sweetheart, love you." Her phone started to buzz with an incoming call. She glanced and saw Patrick's name and picture fill the screen, but she couldn't answer it as she was already drifting off to sleep. Gemma picked it up and took the phone with her back to her own room. "Hey Dad..."

Patrick called back the next morning around nine a.m. her phone was on the kitchen counter. Claire had her hand in yellow, plastic gloves and she was elbow deep in sudsy water. She grabbed the phone and used her face identification to answer it before putting the phone on her shoulder. She hadn't gotten to the dishes the day before and didn't realize how many had accumulated over the past two days.

"Hello," she said juggling the phone in one hand and the pot filled with soapy water in the other.

"Hey babe, it's been forever. I've been trying to reach you," he said.

"I know. I'm sorry. It's been crazy here. I texted you back when I could." They had played phone tag most of the week. Since they kept missing each other, they ended up texting updates on their days instead.

"Yeah, I got your messages. What is all the noise in the background?"

"Oh, I'm doing the dishes because apparently, I'm not organized enough. Brita is on her tablet on the floor next to me. Grayson slept at Kyle's last night and Gemma is still sleeping. I think." *Did I answer his question? I don't even remember what he asked.* "How are you? What's going on in Chi-town."

Patrick began talking, but Claire was only half listening as she finished loading up the dishwasher and washing what was left by hand.

When she was done, she peeled off her gloves and placed them over the faucet head. She found herself saying things like uh. Umm and oh, really. She picked up Brita and the tablet, walked up the stairs to get Brita and herself ready for the day.

Greg and Joss's contribution to helping them out was to have the kids over to their house on Saturday afternoons to play and hang with their cousins. It helped them as well as her kids going over kept their kiddos occupied so they could get stuff done around their own house as well. It was a win-win situation for everyone. "Hold on a second, babe. Brita, Mama's going to put you down so you can get ready to go to Auntie Joss's house."

"Yeah!" Brita exclaimed as she dropped her tablet on the floor and ran to her room. This was why they bought the most expensive outer case covering. It was break-proof or should she say Brita proof. "I'm sorry, babe. Go ahead. Finish what you were saying."

"No, no…it's okay. I want to hear about you and the kids and your week."

"Well, the week was crazy, parent/teacher conferences were fine, and I found out I am an incompetent mother. Other than that, nothing new here." Claire sat down on her unmade bed, placing her arms on her knees while still holding the phone to her ear.

"Oh babe, I don't think that was what they meant. They all want to help, finally. I would think you would be happy about it since they weren't on board with helping in the beginning."

"So obviously you spoke with your mother." She should have known Margie would have called him and given him her side of the story. Especially since she thought Claire would be at work all day yesterday and probably wouldn't be speaking to Patrick until Friday night. Claire still struggled with how involved Margie was in her boys' lives considering she grew up with a mother who was not involved at all.

"Yeah, she called me yesterday late morning." *Bingo! I knew it*. "Their hearts are in the right place, even if it doesn't usually come off that way." *Was he defending her actions?*

"I'm sure," she replied sarcastically, putting the phone on speaker so she could make her bed and get dressed.

"I'm glad your sister is chipping in too. It's about time she did something for someone else other than herself." Claire was getting annoyed with him. They hadn't spoken all week, and this was the last thing she wanted to argue about now that they were finally talking.

"Patrick, that is not fair. I know you are not Becca's biggest fan, but she is a single woman with no children who works eighty-hour weeks. Our children are not her responsibility. Whatever your beef is with her you need to let it go." She threw her pillow to the top of the bed and patted it down. It was easy to make the bed as it was only her side that was slept in most days.

"I'm not saying our kids are her responsibility, but she could at least chip in now and then to offer some support instead of standing there like being with us all is an inconvenience in her life. She also has zero relationship with our kids. You talk about how she was your second mother growing up, but there doesn't seem to be a motherly instinct in her."

"I agree to an extent, but you don't seem to complain about Elana this way. Why is that?" her voice was muffled as she pulled a shirt over her head.

"One, because Elana lives three hours away and can't help. Two, Elana is a lot more likable, and three, when Elana does come for a visit, she always goes above and beyond to spend time with the kids. Becca does nothing with them. Why is that?" He responded to her question with the same question.

She was now hopping around the room trying to put her legs into her pants while standing up. She glanced at the time on the clock trying not to fall over. "Babe, can we talk more about this later. I've got to get Brita over to Joss and Greg's and then pick up the groceries." She was extremely frustrated with him and wanted to end the conversation.

"I thought you were going to start having them delivered?" he asked.

"Boy, your mom really did fill you in on everything. I'll start next week. I already had the order in before my intervention," she said bitterly as she quickly zipped her jeans up and grabbed the cell phone off the bed.

"Claire." She could hear impatience in his voice.

"It's fine, Patrick. I've got to go. I'll talk to you later. Love ya." She didn't wait for a response as she ended the call. She threw herself face down on the bed and screamed into her comforter in frustration.

***

"GEMMA?" CLAIRE POKED HER HEAD INTO HER DAUGHTER'S BEDroom. "I'm taking Brita over to Uncle Greg and Aunt Joss's, do you want to go?"

She heard a mumble or grumble and slowly backed out of the door closing it behind her. Claire called over to Kyle's house next to see if Grayson wanted to go over to his cousin's house. He did. While she waited for him to come home, she loaded Brita into her car seat.

"Where's Daddy?" Brita asked.

"Daddy's in Chicago."

"Did Daddy move there? Joey at school moved and teacher said he has a new house and a new school?" *Out of the mouth of babes.* Claire stared at her in disbelief as she clipped her into her five-point harness.

"No, honey, Daddy didn't move there. He lives here with us. He's there for work. He'll be back next week." Claire closed the sliding van door then climbed into the driver's seat.

"Okay," she said. Little ones had no concept of time so tomorrow or next week were about the same. Grayson came running over from next door and hopped into the seat next to his sister. He gave her hair a tussle with his hand and they both smile at each other. Claire loved seeing them together. She looked in the rear-view mirror at them as Brita was asking her brother a million questions. *I must be doing something right.*

***

CLAIRE WALKED INTO JOSS AND GREG'S HOUSE WITH BAGS HANGing off her arms. *Why am I perpetually carrying so many bags?* "Hello," she yelled out to anyone. Brita and Grayson took off into the house to find their cousins.

"Hi," came Joss's voice from the direction of the kitchen. Claire took her shoes off and headed her way.

"Sorry we're late. Patrick called and I haven't had a chance to talk to him since Wednesday." Joss gave Claire a hug around her ever-growing belly.

"Claire, you never have to apologize to me. It's all good. What do you have there?" Joss wabbled over to her and took one of the bags off of her arm.

She put the rest down on the kitchen table. "I had some bins of Brita's baby clothes I thought I'd bring over in case you could use them."

"Are you kidding me? I thought for sure you would have gotten rid of everything after she grew out of it and Patrick had his vasectomy." Claire laughed at this because it does sound like something she would do. "I guess out of sight out of mind. What time should I pick the kids up? Three?"

"Actually, why don't they stay for dinner tonight? I'm sure you could use some time to yourself." Joss rummaged through the clothes. She pulled out a onesie and laid it across her pregnant belly.

Claire looked at her sister-in-law with her mouth wide open and shock on her face. "Are you kidding me? Have I told you that you are my favorite sister-in-law?"

"I'm your only sister-in-law and of course, I'm sure," Joss said with a laugh. She gave Claire one more hug and shooed her away. Claire found Brita and Grayson in the playroom and gave them both a kiss on the cheek and told them she would see them after dinner.

As she got in the car and began to back out of the driveway, a wave of freedom washed over her. She loved her kids, but she needed this time to herself so badly today. A little time to herself with a to-do list, sort of. She put the car in drive and headed to the grocery store with the radio blaring. It was amazing how much one can get done when they are by themselves. Claire picked up the groceries, unpacked them, and then binge watched a streaming series while folding more laundry. Gemma came down the stairs with her face in her phone. How she didn't trip was beyond Claire.

"Hey sweets, what are you up to today?" Claire looked up from the mounds of laundry piled around herself.

"Can I have a sleepover with a couple of my friends?" Gemma still had not looked up from her phone.

"Possibly, what friends and whose house?" Claire continued folding when she realized Gemma was not going to make eye contact with her.

"Cara and Grace and our house." Gemma walked around the armchair and plopped herself down into it. Head still looking down at her phone.

"Our house," Claire said, turning to her. "Gemma, I'm finally getting caught up on my life and you want to have a sleep over here?"

"Yeah. It's no big deal. We'll hang out in my room the whole time. You won't even know we are here." Claire wasn't convinced. She wanted a quiet weekend.

"Oh, Gem, I don't know. I really need a break." Claire watched as the switch flipped and the devil ears begin to grow. Now Gemma was looking right into her eyes with glaring hatred.

"You never let me do anything. I haven't had friends over here in forever. Ever since Dad left it's like we have no fun anymore, it's always about what needs to be done. I hate it!"

I can't win. "First off, Dad did not leave. He's traveling for work." Claire put the sweatshirt she was folding down to look at Gemma directly.

"Whatever." Gemma stood in a huff, arms crossed at her chest, left hip kicked out in annoyance.

"And you've been busy with play rehearsals so don't make it sound like I'm dragging you all over town with a to-do list in my hand or forcing you to stand at the sink and wash dishes."

"Fine." She said as she plopped herself back down in the armchair sulking. "I just wanted to do something fun this weekend." Claire looked over at her. She was such a sucker. Maybe it wouldn't be so bad letting

Gemma have a sleepover. The girls would entertain each other in Gemma's room. She could spend some extra time with Brita and Grayson too.

"Fine. You can have Cara and Grace over, but you must promise not to destroy the house and the girls need to be picked up by ten a.m. tomorrow morning. Deal?"

"Deal," she said as her demeanor completely changed. She jumped up, kissed Claire on the cheek and ran up the stairs while calling one of them on her phone. "My mom said yes."

I hope I don't regret this. She put the clothes in the basket and headed up the stairs to put them away.

***

"GEMMA," CLAIRE YELLED UP THE STAIRS. "WHAT TIME ARE YOUR friends coming over?"

"Six," she yelled back.

"What do you all want for dinner? I have hot dogs or Bagel Bites."

"We're good. Cara's bringing over stuff for us."

"Okay, I'll be heading to get your brother and sister around then so please tell their parents I'll be right back."

"Got it." Now that Gemma had got her way, things were back to normal. They were yelling across the house to each other, which felt normal to Claire.

I feel so accomplished. Laundry is done and put away, dishes are clean, and the house is in decent shape.

When Claire got to Greg and Joss's house at six o'clock, she couldn't stop hugging both of them and thanking them for having Brita and Grayson over. They said all the kids had the best time and they were both able to get their own weekend chores done. Joss said she even got in a cat nap while watching *Paw Patrol* with Brita and Levi. Wonderful day for everyone.

Driving home through the quiet town streets, Claire looked forward to a mellow Saturday night. However, as Claire was learning, things don't always go how you planned. When they got home, she opened the car door and heard music blaring from the house. The bass was pumping so loud the front door was shaking. *What the hell?*

Grayson opened the front door. The music blasted them all in the face. Claire was surprised the neighbors didn't call the police on them for noise disturbance. She speedwalked over to the stereo and turned it off. "Gemma!" she yelled as she walked into the kitchen. "Oh no, no, no...this is not my kitchen. This is not how it looked when I left." She felt sick to her stomach as she glanced around the room, her knees wanted to give out.

There was flour and pieces of dough all over the kitchen island, red splatters of sauce everywhere like Jackson Pollock painted the kitchen in pizza sauce. Claire looked over at the sink; it was overflowing with dishes. She wanted to cry. She slowly made her way up the stairs and down the hall. She knocked on the door, but the music was too loud for the girls to hear her. She opened the door and stepped inside instead.

"Mom, what the hell? You didn't knock first," Gemma said surprised and mad.

"I did. Your music was so loud you couldn't hear me." She glared at her daughter through gritted teeth. "I'd like to see you out here, please. Hi, girls."

"What is it?" Gemma asked as her two friends looked up at Claire with innocent eyes.

"Out here, please," she said again with the biggest fake smile on her face.

"Fine." Gemma came out into the hallway and closed the door behind her. "What?"

In a whispered voice, Claire said, "What? Is that all you have to say to me? What did I tell you earlier? I did not want a mess. I worked hard all day to get the house in order. In one hour of being gone, you and your friends have completely turned the house upside down."

"Oh my god, Mom. You're so dramatic. It's only a few dishes. We'll do them." Gemma said with an annoyed teenage tone.

"Good, do them now and I want the kitchen to look like it did when I left. Understood." Claire pressed her lips together and tilted her head down, making eye contact with her daughter letting her see how serious she was.

"OMG, you are totally embarrassing me. Can you stop?" Gemma cowered away from Claire's glare.

"Embarrassing you? In front of who? We are in the hallway. There is no one here but the two of us." Claire was losing her patience. She looked up and down the hallway and then back at Gemma.

"Whatever, we'll clean it up." Gemma turned back to her door, escaping back into her room.

"Good," Claire replied, shaking her head. *Twelve-year-olds. The terrible twos of the teen years. I need to go snuggle my baby and make myself feel better.*

"Brita, can Mommy come snuggle you?" she yelled down the hall.

"Yeah, Mommy snuggle time!" her little voice yelled back. Thank goodness for small things.

SIXTEEN

Ten a.m. Sunday morning couldn't arrive fast enough. Claire put on a happy mom face all morning, but she couldn't wait for Gemma's friends to be picked up. She wanted her house to herself. She knew she needed to call Patrick to discuss this new arrangement with the family. She was having so much anxiety even thinking about it. Claire needed to talk to Elana before she could talk to Patrick. She loved that their bills were all being paid now. The stress of that at least was off their shoulders. But now she had to manage the anxiety she felt in anticipation of having the family all up in her business.

Claire decided to wait until both girls were picked up. Standing at the door, she waved goodbye to both moms who were in their cars and headed to the kitchen to pour herself a second cup of coffee. Walking into the living room, she found Grayson playing his video game from his seat on the couch, Brita was on the floor playing with her dolls, and Gemma was slouched over in the armchair. "Hey guys, I'm going to call Auntie Laney. Are you all good? Grayson and Gemma, can you keep an eye on Brita?"

"I'm tired. I'm going back to bed," Gemma said.

"Yeah, Mom. I got her," he said, shaking his head in annoyance at his older sister. Claire smiled at him and then watched Gemma climb the stairs up to her room. Sadness took over Claire. She suddenly felt very lonely.

She walked out of the room and back to the little nook in the kitchen. They had a wraparound bench on two sides of their eat-in kitchen table. Claire loved sitting in the corner with her back against the cushions and feet spread out on the long bench. The warm sun came in through the windows at this time of day. It felt so good for her to soak up some vitamin D. She crawled into the spot with her cell phone in one hand while putting the coffee cup on the table.

"Hi sis," Elana said when she picked up after two rings. As soon as Claire heard her voice, she choked up and couldn't speak. "Claire, I'm here. Honey, you're stronger than you think you are." That was it. The flood gates open and Claire began to cry.

"Am I though?" she said through her tears. She was holding onto the tightness in her chest, so she didn't turn into a blubbering mess. She also didn't want the kids to hear her.

"You are sis. You really are. I know the thought of people helping you makes you uncomfortable, you are used to doing things yourself, but you need to be okay with it. We all love you. Remember everything is coming from a place of love. We love you. Patrick loves you. The kids love you. You're going to be okay."

"I know. They made me feel like I am failing my family. Margie in my house helping to clean up and do laundry stresses me out. It's such an invasion of our privacy. I don't want her folding my underwear and bras."

Elana laughed on the other end.

"I wouldn't want that either. Tell her that. Actually, text her. That way you can avoid confrontation. What if instead, they pick up Brita and bring her home so you can come home from work and do other things? Maybe get a few minutes to yourself."

"I don't want to ask them to commit to five afternoons a week. I also like my drives home with Brita. She fills me in on all the events from her day. You know, who pooped themselves, who was not being a nice friend, and who she played with that day. I like our time together."

"Then give it this week with Margie in the house and set some boundaries. Tell her you'd appreciate her doing the kids' laundry, but she doesn't need to do yours. Tell her she doesn't need to clean the house, but if she wants to put the dishes in the dishwasher away you'd appreciate it. You start the dishwasher before school, and she can unload when she gets to your house." Claire could tell Elana was trying to downplay the situation as she knew this would be a big adjustment for her. Claire also knew she could use the help and needed to get comfortable allowing other people into the four walls she had built up around herself and her family.

"Why do you make it seem so easy? Will you text what you just said to me so I can copy and paste it in a text to her? That would make my life easier right there."

Elana was laughing at her again.

"You are so ridiculous and yes, I'll text it to you. Now tell me about Becca. How was she? What is her role in all of this?" Claire gazed out the window as she thought about their interaction before Becca left the house Thursday night.

"You know, Laney. I don't get her at all. It's like she needs Margie's approval more than mom's. She was in full lawyer mode treating my intervention like she was assigned to the case."

"Sounds about right. It's how she deals with uncomfortable situations," Elana said.

"She's going to pick Gemma up from her play rehearsals and bring her home. The weird thing is Gemma didn't give me a tough time about not carpooling with her friends anymore. She thinks Becca is misunderstood. Maybe she's seeing something I'm not. The strangest thing from the whole night was the absence of Mom. I've even texted her and still haven't heard back." Claire had sent her mom a quick text just asking her how she was feeling. She thought maybe Justine was sick since she wasn't at the house on Thursday night.

Claire heard Elana clear her throat. "Claire, Mom isn't Margie's biggest fan. She makes her feel uncomfortable." Claire knew this. Margie had a big personality and Justine did as well, but in a different way. Margie was the overly involved in her children's lives type of mother while Justine was more about setting high expectations for her girls on how they behaved. She genuinely could have used her mom to stand up for her as a mom in that moment. For a long time, she was like a single parent with her father's long workdays. One would think her mom would be more supportive of what Claire was going through. Claire felt she needed her mom, not her mother-in-law. It should not have surprised Claire her mother was not there for her when she needed her. The little girl in her always held out hope one day her mother would surprise her and be the mom Claire wished she needed her to be.

"Also," Elana continued, "she's second guessing selling the house. She's struggling with the change."

Claire almost spit out the sip of coffee she just took. "What? Why is this the first time I'm hearing about this?"

"You've been so busy; we didn't want to bother you. The junk removal company they hired came to help them clear out the basement and attic about a week and a half ago. She sent them away. Then she called Becca crying, Becca texted me and we decided to let it go. You know how Mom is with change. She's not ready, Claire." Claire was in disbelief that nobody thought to fill her in on this change. Just another example of her feeling left out of her own family.

"No one is making them downsize. I thought this was what they wanted?" She pinched the bridge of her nose.

"Theoretically, they like the idea of having less house to take care of and no yard work. When it comes down to it, she's not ready to leave her home. Dad thinks she'll change her mind again. She needs to get comfortable letting go of all the old stuff and moving into a new place." Claire could hear her sisters tone softening. She was speaking to Claire like a little kid who was not understanding her words.

"I understand completely. I don't understand why I'm finding out about it a week and half later?" Claire sat back in the little nook saddened by how left out she felt.

"Claire don't get defensive. We didn't want to bother you. You have enough going on within your own house. Becca hired a teenager to mow the lawn for them and we found a reasonably priced housecleaner to do the deep cleaning once a month. We'll see how mom feels in a couple of months and then they can reevaluate selling. It's all taken care of." Elana's tone shifted to reassurance. Claire was done with this conversation. She had called Elana in hopes of feeling better about her new situation starting that week. Instead, she felt worse.

"Okay," Claire said defeated. "Thank you both for helping them out. I should let you go. I need to call Patrick and then start getting ready for the week ahead. Talk to you Friday morning for our coffee talk." She hung up before Elana could respond. A wave of disappointment washed over her. The plates were falling, and she couldn't catch them. Tears formed on her eyelashes and a lump formed in her throat. She knew she needed to call Patrick, but she was too drained to do it then. All Claire wanted to do was hide away from life for a little while. She scooched herself out of her corner, put her mug inside the dishwasher and headed into the living room.

"Who wants to go for a little trip in the car?" she asked Grayson and Brita.

"Ice cream?" Brita asked. That's all Claire needed to hear to put a smile back on her face.

"Yes, sweet pea, ice cream too." *Mint chocolate chip always makes me feel better.*

"Yeah!" Brita jumped up from the floor and into Claire's arms. Then she screamed at the top of her lungs. "Gemma! Where going out for ice cream!" *Ice cream for lunch it is!*

***

PATRICK AND CLAIRE HAD BEEN PLAYING PHONE TAG AGAIN. They had barely spoken more than a handful of words to each other since Saturday morning. The physical and emotional distance from each other seemed the same to Claire at this point, thousands of miles in between. Tuesday afternoon came and Claire picked Brita up from daycare. Today was the first day of the new schedule with her mother-in-law. She headed home dreading what she would find. She texted Margie what she and Elana had talked about on Sunday. Margie responded with an *OK*.

Claire pulled into the driveway; her dad was not home with Grayson yet and Gemma was still at play practice. Claire got Brita out of her car seat and grabbed her armful of work bags. She slowly walked up to the big, wooden front door, inserted the key, and turned it. *Why am I so afraid to go into my own house?* Gently opening the door, she immediately noticed it smelled amazing inside. It was a mix of cleaner and roast. She and Brita headed into the kitchen. Claire placed her bags on the kitchen island along with Brita's backpack. She headed to the pantry for goldfish. There was a note on the counter.

Claire,

I made a roast with vegetables. It's in the oven already cooked, it just needs to be reheated. There is enough for a couple of nights of dinner for you and the kids. The dishes are put away and the kid's laundry is on their beds in their rooms so they can put them away themselves. Have a good night.

Love,

Margie

Claire looked around the kitchen. It was so nice and clean. In awe, she walked around the house like she was noticing it for the first time. The living room was picked up and vacuumed. She walked up the stairs and down the hall. All the kids' beds were made, and their laundry was on their beds waiting to be put away. They each had a note on their bed which said,

Make your bed before you go to school. I'll be checking. Grams

What is happening right now? Claire thought she might cry. She peeked into her closed bedroom door, and it was exactly as she left it. *Hallelujah! Maybe this is going to work out after all.*

SEVENTEEN

Becca was sitting outside the front of the middle school waiting for Gemma to get out of play rehearsal. The front door kept opening and different groups of kids came pouring out, but no Gemma.

Becca kept looking at the seventh graders trying to remember herself at that age. She remembered having a close group of friends she hung out with and would have sleepovers with, and they also talked way too much about boys. She avoided having them over to her house because she was always forced to include her sisters, or rather take care of them while her friends were over. She was awkward, had just gotten her period, and started wearing a training bra. All the weirdness happens in middle school, and she couldn't share it with her sisters. They were too little. Her mom had told her to talk to her friends about it and not her sisters, which was fine with Becca since her friends were going through these changes too.

Gemma was in one of the last groups to exit the school. She was laughing and looked so at ease and happy. Becca saw her look up and smile at her and give her a wave of her hand. Then Gemma waved goodbye to her friends and headed over to Becca's car.

"Hey, Aunt Becca, thanks for picking me up," she said as she made her way into the front seat with her backpack still on her back.

"Do you want to put your backpack in the backseat?" Becca pointed to the space behind the passenger seat.

"Nah, I'm good. We're just going home." Gemma hunched over while putting on her seat belt.

"That doesn't look very comfortable." Becca put the car in drive and started heading down the street. She was trying to think of something to say to Gemma. She couldn't remember if she'd ever had a one-on-one conversation with her or not.

"How was school?" she asked glancing over at her niece.

"Good," Gemma replied while glancing out the passenger side window.

Becca was trying to think of something else to ask. "And play practice?"

"Fine."

One-word answers, Becca thought how she used to be the same way with adults when she was that age. "What play are you doing?" she asked while take a left hand turn out of the school parking lot.

"Peter Pan." Gemma finally turned her head to her aunt.

"Oh, which part are you playing?" Becca tried to sound enthusiastic. Theatre was not her thing.

"I'm not in it. I work backstage. I'm part of the set crew." She saw a huge smile spread across Gemma's face. She could see her niece took pride in her work on the play.

"Oh, that's nice." *That's nice?* Dumbest conversation ever. They rode along in silence until they came upon the horse farm.

"Over there is where I keep my horses," Becca said, pointing toward the barn outside the passenger window.

"What? You have horses?" Gemma turned to look at the barn. There were a few horses out in the field grazing. "How did I not know you have horses? How many do you have?" Gemma asked.

"I board two horses there. Winnie and Rascal. I usually go in the morning to see them before work and then take them out riding on the weekends."

"You ride horses," Gemma said surprised.

"Yes," Becca said smiling now. "I ride horses. I took lessons when I was a kid and started back up when you were about two years old."

"Wow. I never knew. Can I go with you sometime? Can I meet them, and you can teach me how to ride?" Gemma's full attention was now on her. Becca was happy her niece was showing some interest in her.

"You would want to do that?" she asked.

"Hell yeah, I would." They both laughed together.

"Okay, then *hell yeah*, I'll take you one Saturday." Becca finished the ride back to Claire's house with a smile on her face. She made a connection with her niece, and it felt good. It also opened up the conversation and Gemma began to tell her everything that happened in her day and at rehearsal. Becca didn't realize how animated Gemma was. She then told Gemma all about her horses and how she came to own them, answering Gemma's million questions.

EIGHTEEN

"Mom! I'm home." Gemma ran into the house slamming the front door behind her.

Claire came into the living room from the kitchen drying her hands on a dish towel. "Hey sweets, how was rehearsal? Dinner is in the microwave waiting for you."

Gemma dropped her backpack on the floor and headed over to the microwave. "Did you know Aunt Becca owns two horses?"

"Yeah, Rascal and something," she said walking back over to the counter that she had been wiping down.

"Winnie. Rascal and Winnie. She said I could go with her one Saturday to meet them." Gemma pressed the buttons on the microwave to heat up her dinner. Claire looked over at Gemma dumbfounded. *Becca invited Gemma to the farm.* She was pleasantly surprised by how this day was working out. She was excited to talk to Patrick and tell him all about it, something good to share.

"Let's call Dad. He should be out of work by now." She reached for her cell phone. She had each of the kids take a turn speaking with him before she took her turn. She filled him in on the events of the day.

"I am so happy to hear how great it worked out, babe. You sound more at ease than you have in a long time. See, we can accept help," Patrick said, and she imagined in her mind's eye the side smirk on his lips.

"I'm slowly learning to be okay with it." They talked for another half hour before he needed to go out to dinner with colleagues. It was nice to catch up on life with him without her feeling a tad resentful of the situation. They agreed they needed a date night that weekend and she typed into her notes app to make a reservation for Saturday for them. She would need to figure out a place for them to go first. Claire fell asleep that night feeling more relaxed than she had in an exceptionally long time.

The rest of the week moved along smoothly. Claire felt like she had turned a corner. Patrick got home Friday night. The kids were ecstatic to see him. Per their request, Gemma and Grayson didn't make plans with friends so they could have family time. Patrick gave her the biggest hug when he walked in the house, and it felt like all of the tension which had been building up between them washed away in the physical connection of that hug. Claire's heart was full seeing her family together again.

Claire and Patrick had dinner at their favorite bar and grille on Saturday night. The kids all went to Joss and Greg's while they had their date night. "This is exactly what I needed," Claire said as they clinked their beer glasses together.

"Me too," Patrick leaned across the table and gave her a kiss before taking a swig of beer from his pint glass. "I feel like I haven't looked at your face in ages. I like seeing your face."

"I like seeing yours too," she said a little flirtatiously. They needed this night out to reconnect. It had been a long time coming. "I want to hear all about you, how the project is going, how you are doing, and then maybe the last thing we will talk about tonight is our kids." She laughed, and Patrick joined in.

"Sounds good." He smiled over at her. They spent the next two hours chatting and laughing. They reminisced about their early days together living in their small one-bedroom apartment where they would bump butts just trying to walk past each other. They joked about moving from the small apartment to their small house and how huge it felt when they first moved in until they filled it with children. Claire looked over at him as he paid the bill and felt like they were returning to the Claire and Patrick she loved. Her partner in life. She felt such attraction to him in that moment she wondered if she was still nimble enough to have a quickie in the car. "I know that look." He said when they made eye contact. She sheepishly smiled at him. He grabbed her hand, and they headed out the door.

When they finally arrived back at Greg and Joss's house, after a quick stop at home, the kids were finishing up a movie in the family room. The two couples sat on adjacent couches in the living room and chatted.

"So, truthfully," Joss said to Claire. "How did the week go?"

"Actually, not so bad. Margie was surprisingly a huge help, picking up from our morning and making us dinner that lasted a couple of nights. Becca picking up Gemma worked out great. I didn't have to drag Brita back out. Becca even told Gemma she would take her to the farm to meet her horses."

"Oh, we love Rascal and Winnie. They are the sweetest horses and so good with the kids." Joss was making circles on her pregnant belly as she spoke.

Claire stared in shock at both Greg and Joss. "You've met my sister's horses?"

"Sure," Greg said. "Becca has let us stop by a bunch of times on the weekends when she's there. The kids brush them, fill their water, and even help scoop out the poop from their stall. Occasionally, the kids will get to exercise them around the ring too."

"How is this the first I'm hearing about this? Our kids have never met her horses," she said dumbfounded.

"This surprises you?" Patrick asked with little surprise in is voice. "I've told you. She doesn't bother with her nieces and nephew. You should talk to her about this, babe. I'm sure our kids would like to meet the horses too."

"I don't understand why she's never brought it up." Claire tried to think if there was a time Becca had invited her kids to the farm, but she couldn't recall of one unless she just forgot about it.

Joss looked at Greg and then at me. "No offense, guys. But it's not like you try to have a relationship with Becca at all. It's not just on her. She's your immediate family...and you only see Becca once a month at family dinners. *You* keep her at arm's length." Sometimes Claire loved how blunt Joss could be and other times it was a bit overwhelming for her, this was one of those times.

"No, we don't," she said as she made eye contact with each of them. "Do we?"

Greg glanced over at her. "I don't want to get in the middle of anything. There is a lot more to Becca than we see at family gatherings. You'd be surprised if you spent some one-on-one time with her."

"You guys spend one on one time with her?" Claire had no idea what was going on right now. She felt like she had entered an alternate reality.

"Well, yeah. She gets tickets and things through work and invites us to go or will give them to us so we can have a night out and she'll stay with the kids."

"Wait a minute," Patrick was shaking his head in disbelief. "She watches your kids." Joss and Greg looked at each other like they realized they had said too much. "Why does she watch your kids and not ours?"

"Because we ask," Joss said sheepishly, shrugging. Claire could tell she wanted to get out of this conversation as soon as possible. "The first time she offered us free tickets to a movie premiere she got through work we told her we'd love to go but we didn't have a sitter. She said she hated horror movies and would happily watch the kids so we could go. She didn't want to see the tickets go to waste. It was a win-win situation. We got a date night out and the horror flick, which we both love, and she took the kids over to meet Rascal and Winnie."

"We hate horror movies," Claire said under her breath.

"Becca knows that which was why she offered them to us. Please don't make a big thing out of this you guys. Really, it was a fluke thing that worked out," Greg said. Claire could tell he was trying to keep the peace by making light of the situation.

"Yeah, fine," Patrick said. He liked to keep the peace too, so it was easier for him to drop things, but Claire knew it would come back up at another time.

***

Claire hadn't seen her mother in a couple of weeks. It was really bothering her that her mother still hadn't shown up for the night of her intervention or responded to her text. On Sunday, she decided to drop in to see her without calling first. She knew how much her mom hated it when people didn't call first, but Claire was afraid if she called first her mom would tell her to stay home with Patrick and the kids.

Her parents lived one town over from them. It took about fifteen minutes to drive over to their house, which gave her time to formulate her thoughts. Claire loved the neighborhood she grew up in and could understand why her mom didn't want to leave it. All the streets had sidewalks for walking, running, or biking on. Everyone in town took loving care of their homes and lawns. There was no bad side of the town. With it being early March, buds began to bloom on the trees and the crocuses were popping their heads up out of the ground thanks to the mild winter they had.

Claire pulled up to her childhood home. Her parents were the second owners of the house. The first owners were only in it for two years before the husband got transferred for his job. It was like moving into a brand-new home.

Claire parked in front of the house and made her way up the walkway. Her father opened the front door after one knock. "Claire bear, what a nice surprise," he said with a warm smile on his face as he rested his hands on his big belly. Everything about her father was comforting. His broad shoulders, welcoming smile and salt and pepper hair that always looked windblown. She walked up the two steps, meeting him at the doorway. "Hey Dad, is mom around?" He moved out of the way for her to enter the house.

"Sure is, come on in." Walking into their home was like stepping back in time. They needed to update most of the rooms. "She's out back puttering around in the garden beds. Hope you don't mind if I stay here and finish watching the hockey game."

"No, of course not," she said laughing at him. This was typical of her father. His favorite sports teams took precedence over anything else going on. Claire made her way through the kitchen and sliding glass doors to find her mother sitting in an Adirondack chair with gardening gloves on and a sun hat covering her head. "Hey, Mom."

Her mom turned her head around to see who it was. "Claire? What are you doing here?"

"I haven't seen you in a while. I wanted to stop by and see how you were doing?"

"You should be home with Patrick and the kids," she said. "But since you're here, come on over and take a seat. I finished clearing out the back garden beds. I'm taking a breather before I start on the ones by the side of the house."

Claire walked over and sat in the chair opposite Justine. It was serene in their backyard with all the flower beds and greenery. They'd done an impressive job of making the backyard look like an English garden. There were a variety of colors waiting to pop as the temperatures got warmer. "Elana told me you guys decided you're not going to sell the house."

"We will one day. Not right now. We're not ready to leave this place," she said, sweeping her arm over the yard and house.

"I get that. Elana told me Becca found a teenager to mow the lawn and they got you a housecleaner to do the deep clean once a month." Claire looked at her mother to see if she had any kind of reaction to this new change. Her mom was never good at relinquishing control in her own home.

"Yes, the boy is great. The housecleaner is going to have to take some getting used to. I'm not so comfortable with someone coming in and being all in my things." Justine fiddled with the sunhat on her head. Finally, she took it off and placed it in her lap.

"That's how I feel about Margie coming over and helping at my house." Claire glanced over at her mother to trying to get a read on her. She didn't see any change in her demeanor. "It's weird."

"Well, that's because you don't know how to take help from others. You never have. Always wanting to do things by yourself. Be in control of it all." She took her gardening gloves off and massaged her arthritic hands.

"Maybe because I had no other choice growing up," she said under her breath. Her mother chose to ignore the comment. "Can I ask you something?" she said, nervously twisting her hands in her lap. Justine looked over at her. "The night everyone was at my house. What I keep calling my 'intervention,' why weren't you there?"

She looked down at her hands and then up at Claire "I didn't want to be involved. It was Margie's show." She sighed. "I have no issues with Margie, I really don't. She can be a bit much at times, but I know her heart is in the right place. You and Patrick are great parents, and you are doing right by your family. I don't feel we should get involved unless *you* feel you need it. Dad loves spending time with Grayson. I don't want to be in your business."

Claire thought about this for a moment. "Surprisingly, it was helpful having her help out a couple of days this week and having Becca picking up Gemma from rehearsal."

"So having people support you when you need it is helpful. Is that what you are saying?" She was making fun of Claire now.

"Yes." She smiled and nodded at her mother. "Did you know Becca hangs out with Joss and Greg, babysits their kids sometimes, and even takes them to see the horses?"

"Sure. Rascal and Winnie are her children. They are her outlet to escape her busy work schedule. Joss's kids love going to visit them." Claire's heart sank. It was like her family had a whole other relationship outside of her and her immediate family.

"I don't understand. Why has she never brought my kids over to meet them? Last week she was bringing Gemma home from rehearsal and they drove by the farm. Becca invited Gemma to go meet her horses one Saturday. That was the first time, and Gemma is twelve." Claire was trying to make sense in her mind about all that was happening without her knowledge.

"Claire, you and Patrick are pretty closed off to the rest of us. You are very protective of the kids. You keep them wrapped up in your tight family bubble. You don't leave much room in your life for her to have a place in theirs. There's always something to do or some place to be or you need your family time. Sometimes we all feel like an obligation." She spoke to her in that stern motherly voice she knew all too well from growing up. She felt like she was being reprimanded by her mother.

"An obligation!" She was shocked. Her family thought she saw *them* as an obligation. She felt like she was the obligation. The third child, not wanted, not expected, the unplanned pregnancy that ruined the future her mother had planned for herself after her older sisters went to school full time.

"Those Sunday dinners you and Patrick organized and started, I appreciate you including Dad and I, but we could do without them. We get together every month. We rotate houses. It's exhausting. Taking a month off here and there would be nice now and then." She watched her mother swipe away at the dirt on her pants.

"Why is this the first I'm hearing of this? We thought it would be nice to have traditional family dinners where everyone could see each other. A nice tradition to have for the kids to remember. Does Becca feel this way too?" she asked.

"I think Becca feels completely out of place, especially with everything that happened with Patrick's Uncle Frank." Justine looked at Claire soberly like this is information she should know about and understand.

"What do you mean? What happened with Patrick's Uncle Frank?" Claire stood from her chair and started pacing around on the plush, green grass while picking at her cuticles.

"Oh, my goodness, Claire. Have you been living under a rock? Margie set Becca up with George's youngest brother, Frank. It was a complete disaster. Margie blames Becca and Becca feels awkward about it, so she does whatever Margie asks to keep the peace. Ask Patrick about it. I'm sure he knows more than I do." Claire stopped in her tracks and turned to face her mother.

"Becca? Dated Uncle Frank? There's like a fifteen-year age gap. How did I not know this? Why didn't Becca tell me? I assumed she was too busy working to date." Once again, she felt left out of her own family. She felt like everyone was either conspiring against her to keep her in the dark or were just choosing not to include her because it was what her family always did.

Justine stood up from her chair and walked over to Claire. "Claire, call your sister, take her out to lunch, get to know her. You all used to be so close when you were younger."

"And whose fault was that, Mom? It's not like you ever tried to foster a relationship between you and the three of us. You punished Becca and then Elana once they got their period by separating us all. You left us all to care for ourselves when we were little and then it was like becoming a woman was a sin or something and we were pulled apart. Now look at us. You wonder why I can't ask for help; it is because I was left on my own once they moved out. You were never there for me once they were gone." Claire tried not to get emotional, but she could feel tears of sadness and anger creeping in.

"Oh, stop being so dramatic." Her mother walked over to the side table waving her off. Justine picked up her gardening gloves she had placed there and began putting them back on. "I did the best I could. Your father worked all the time. I raised you three girls, other people's children, and then worked in your father's office. I took care of everyone and now it's my turn to take care of me, you girls can manage your own relationships. You are all grown adults now. And look, you all turned out just fine."

"We turned out fine? Becca is married to her job, Elana moved to the

Cape to get away from you and your judgmental eye, and I'm... I'm... well, I don't even know what I am." Claire's face was turning red, and she was beginning to sweat from her anger and frustration.

"So, it's my fault you girls grew apart. You still talk to Elana; Becca is one town over. No one is standing in your way. It's time to stop blaming me for things that have gone wrong in your life." Justine turned away from Claire as if the conversation were over. Claire followed right behind her.

"I'm not saying that—actually yes, that's exactly what I'm saying. Becca has spent most of her life trying to meet your standards, Elana moved away so she could live her life the way she wanted to without your input and I'm trying to raise my kids to feel the love from their mother that we never felt from you." Claire was shocked by the words coming out of her own mouth. She couldn't believe she was speaking to her mother this way and yet, she was not sorry.

"So, I was a bad mother? Claire, I would think, out of you three, you would understand what it's like trying to do it all on your own without your husband around to help. Jeez, Claire, get over yourself," Justine said, turning away from her and walking over to the garden bed next to the French doors. Claire followed her.

"Mom, you're not listening to me. I'm not saying you were a bad mother. There were many times I would have liked comfort from *you* instead of Laney or Becca. I wish I could have turned to my mom for advice or a hug when I needed one. That wasn't who you were. I'm grateful you're like that with your grandchildren, but I missed having it for me. It was Becca who got your attention and then it went to the other kids and then there was nothing left for Elana or me."

"Oh Claire, you're so naive. How is my parenting any different than your own? You are doing your best just as I did. You focus your attention on Brita so much Gemma gets lost in the mix. It happens. You're lucky Grayson is so easygoing and couldn't care less. Wait and you'll see. It will shift as Gemma gets older and starts testing you like Becca did to us. You'll realize there is only so much you can do as a parent until you have to let your kids become their own person. With Patrick being gone so much for work, I would think you would understand what life was like for me better. We do our best with the hand we are dealt." This conversation was over for Justine.

She squeezed Claire's hand and turned away from her, going back to her gardening. Claire stood there stunned. She felt like she needed to reevaluate her whole family dynamic. Had she and Patrick been so self-absorbed with their family of five they'd neglected the rest of their family? Now that she was taking care of her three kids mostly on her own, she felt her perspective on the way she was raised might be shifting. Maybe she had not given her mother enough credit. Claire realized she had a lot to think about.

We do the best we can, right? Am I turning into my mother with my own kids? Were they being left to care for themselves? Do they feel like I am neglecting them the way I felt I was neglected? I don't take care of other people's children in my house, but I do in my classroom.

NINETEEN

Driving home, Claire had so many thoughts going through her head. Becca dated Patrick's Uncle Frank? Claire naively didn't even know she dated, never mind Frank. She knew she should take her mom's advice and call Becca. The thought of it made her feel so uncomfortable, they hadn't had that kind of relationship in an extraordinarily long time. She couldn't remember the last time she had actually spoken on the phone with her sister that didn't involve a task or a family event.

She called Patrick on the way home to see if she needed to pick anything up before coming home. She asked him about Becca and Frank. "I don't understand how I did not know about their relationship. She's my sister. He's your uncle."

"We had little kids at the time. We were lost in our own world. Babe, I wouldn't overthink it." She knew he was trying to ease her guilt, but she still felt guilty, nonetheless. She now wondered if she had neglected her sister. "They only dated for a few months after Grayson was born. Frank was looking for a wife and mother for his children. Becca was not interested. It ended before it started. It was all my mom's doing. Becca told Mom she didn't need a man in her life to be happy. Mom was upset with her for Frank's sake. That was that." Claire assumed this must be why Becca didn't talk much when she was around Margie but did everything she asked to please her. Not at all the relationship she thought her sister had all this time with her mother-in-law.

Claire didn't know how she missed so much at the time. All she remembered from that time was how Grayson was a colicky baby and she was exhausted. She guessed it made sense they were wrapped up in their own world.

As she drove down the tree-lined streets, she made a commitment to herself to do better for her family, her whole family. *I will put more effort into my relationship with my sister. I will be more open to accepting help from others. I need to let go of the past.* Her stomach turned as she said these affirmations in her head.

***

THE FOLLOWING EVENING AS SHE AND THE KIDS SAT DOWN TO dinner, Claire looked at both of her girls wondering if what her mother said was true. Did she overcompensate with Brita to make up for the lack of love she felt from her parents? Since Brita was born, had she left Gemma to fend for herself like her mother did to them?

As she laid in bed that night, Claire's thoughts perseverated on the conversation from yesterday with her mother. Her cell phone rang, and she reached over and saw Patrick's name and face illuminating. "Do I play favorites with Brita over Gemma?"

"Hi to you too. I'm well. Work was good today." She could hear his amusement coming through the receiver.

"Patrick, listen. When I was at my parent's house yesterday and talking to my mom, she more or less told me I favor Brita over Gemma and leave Grayson to float by in his own happy world." She sat up in bed ready to have a serious discussion about this with her husband.

"Claire, first off Justine is not someone you should be taking motherly advice from. Second, Brita is four years old and still needs us to help her with many of her daily living needs. Gemma is twelve and a very capable pre-teen." Claire listened while chewing on the side of her nail. She played around with what he was saying in her head. "I guess. She made me feel so guilty."

"Again, you're taking parenting advice from Justine. This was a woman who took care of other people's children while completely neglecting her own. Because she was paid to do it, not out of love for those kids." Claire hated and loved when he was so right. He always knew how to make her feel better.

"You're right. Okay, I'm done thinking about it," she said fully knowing she was not. "Tell me about your day." She snuggled back into her bed, closed her eyes, and let him talk, pretending he was lying next to her.

The next morning, as they were rushing around the kitchen, Claire grabbed Gemma in a big hug and said into her ear. "Gemma, have I been showing you enough love? Have I been ignoring you?"

Gemma stood there with her arms at her side. "What's happening right now?"

"I want to make sure you know I love you just as much as your brother and sister." Claire squeezed her a bit tighter as she spoke.

"O-kay." Gemma still stood there stiff as a board.

"Do you think I give more attention to Brita than I do to you?" Claire asked her as she pulled away to look Gemma directly in the eyes.

"Of course, you do. But she's four and she's a hot mess. If you didn't, she'd be running around the house naked covered in baby powder screaming, I'm Grandma." Gemma pulled away and threw the strap of her backpack over her shoulder. "Are we good now? I have to go catch the bus?"

"Yes," Claire said, smiling. "Love you. Have a wonderful day."

Gemma murmured, "Love you too," while walking out the door. At least Claire thought or hoped she did.

She turned to the breakfast table. Grayson was staring at her. "Parents are so weird," he said before shoving another spoonful of cereal into his mouth. Claire walked over to the table, hugged him from behind and began smothering him in kisses. He tried to escape her grasp while laughing at the same time.

"Mama, are you weird?" Brita asked her while sitting on the floor with her bowl of cereal between her legs.

"Yes, Brita. Yes, I am."

TWENTY

The end of March and beginning of April came and went like boats in a harbor. Claire and the kids were in a better rhythm at home. She was also feeling less overwhelmed by her life. Her students were getting spring fever as April vacation approached. It was hard to keep them engaged in lessons when they could feel the sun shining through the classroom windows and the cool breeze coming in. Early Spring had arrived.

Claire was feeling more confident in herself. After work, she made herself a cup of chamomile tea and headed out to the backyard with Brita. She took the cover off of the sandbox and raked the sand around to soften it up a bit. Brita was excited to play in her sandbox again with her trucks, buckets, and shovels. Claire pulled a chair up next to the sandbox watching her play. She had been contemplating calling Becca for a few days. *Rip the Band-Aid off, Claire.* She grabbed her phone out of her back pocket with one hand while placing her cup of tea on the little side table next to her with the other hand.

As she opened her phone, the uncomfortable feeling in her stomach returned. She pushed it down, found Becca's name in her phone, and called her. It was five, Claire assumed she was at work. *Well, maybe I can leave a message. That would be a nice first step.* She pressed send and listened to the phone ringing once, twice...

"Hello," Becca answered, sounding a bit panicky.

"Um...Becca, it's Claire."

"I know. Caller ID. What's up? Is everything okay? Are Mom and Dad, okay? Did Gemma's rehearsal time change?" she responded in her rapid-fire lawyer voice.

"No, no. I was calling to say hi and to see how you are doing?" Claire could hear how awkward she sounded in her head. She realized she was nervous.

There was silence on the other end to the point where the air grew extremely uncomfortable. *Maybe I should have started with a text first. Why do I have such a tough time talking to my own sister?*

"I'm good, you?" Becca responded hesitantly.

I need to think of something to talk about.

"I'm good. This new routine you all came up with seems to be working out nicely. Thank you for helping to organize it." Becca didn't respond. Claire couldn't tell if it was because she was distracted with work or if she was trying to figure out if this was why she called. Claire thought quickly. "Gemma told me you invited her to meet your horses one Saturday. I think that's great. I know she would really enjoy it. Grayson and Brita would love to meet them sometime too."

She heard her sister let out a breath of air as if she finally understood why Claire called. "Of course, of course. How about this Saturday? I can pick up Gemma around seven a.m. and she can come to the stables with me. Let her meet them on her own first, since that's what I told her initially, and then I can bring Grayson and Brita over another time."

Claire agreed even though she knew getting Gemma up and ready for seven a.m. on a Saturday would not be fun. They ended their conversation and Claire put her phone back in her back pocket.

"Who was that, Mommy?" Brita asked.

"Aunt Becca," she said as she got up from her chair and joined Brita in the sandbox for a little sensory therapy.

"She's a grumpy bird," Brita responded. Claire looked down at her youngest.

"Well, she owns two horses and offered for you guys to go over to the barn, meet them and maybe even ride them sometime." Claire knew she was embellishing a little. It was time she started to mend this relationship for the whole family.

"Really?" Brita's eyes lit up. "I love horses." Claire smiled at her daughter while running her fingers through the cool sand.

TWENTY-ONE

Becca was sitting in her office staring at her cell phone. She swiveled back and forth in her leather chair. That was a strange phone call, she thought to herself. It was like Claire called for one reason and then changed the topic to another. Becca shrugged it off. She was looking forward to Saturday with Gemma at the farm. Gemma had been more conversational with her since the first time she picked her up from rehearsal. She's sharing more about school and the friends she hangs out with. Becca felt like she was getting to know her niece better with these short trips home.

It had also been good for her as well as it made her leave the office at a decent hour. No more burning the midnight oil. Even if she had more work to do, at least she went home, poured herself a glass of wine, made herself dinner, and then finished up anything still needing her attention. She felt a little lighter with this new arrangement. Gemma was a great kid. Spending some one-on-one time with Grayson and Brita without the family around would be nice too. She took her cell phone off her desk and began typing a message to Elana.

Claire called me out of the blue.

Is everything okay?

Yeah. She asked if Brita and Grayson could come meet my girls sometime too. Gemma is coming this Saturday.

That's great.

It is, isn't it?

Yes :0)

TWENTY-TWO

Claire told Gemma the plan for Saturday when she got home that night. She was incredibly excited. She didn't even flinch when Claire told her what time Becca would be picking her up. Claire was at the kitchen island packing lunches for the next day, and they were chatting in the kitchen. Gemma had a huge smile on her face, and she even came around the island and half hugged her. Claire was shocked. It was rare to get a spontaneous hug from her. Brita was on a stool at the island playing with her red Play-Doh. She asked if she could go meet the horses too on Saturday." Claire looked at Gemma and saw her face drop. "Not this time, sweet pea. You'll get to meet them another time. This time is for Gemma." She glanced over at Gemma from the corner of her eye while packing Brita's bento box and saw the smile return to her face. *Win for Mom. I'll take it.*

TWENTY-THREE

Becca arrived at Claire's house at seven a.m. Gemma was sitting on the front steps dressed exactly as Becca had suggested she should on Thursday night. She wore old jeans, hiking boots, and brought a sweatshirt since it's cold at the farm early in the morning. Gemma jumped up from the step and ran down to the car. Becca could see the excitement on her face as she got in and buckled her seatbelt.

"Good morning," she said. "I grabbed us coffee. I wasn't sure what you took in yours, so I had them add cream and sugar." She handed Gemma the cardboard cup. Gemma looked surprised and said thanks. It occurred to Becca she didn't know if Gemma drank or was even allowed to drink coffee.

She looked at Gemma as she took a sip. "That's good. It's hot, but good. Thank you." Why does this little validation from a twelve-year old feel so good to Becca? She wasn't sure and she was excited for the day ahead with her niece. They spent the morning at the stables. Becca showed Gemma how to clean the stalls, feed and brush the horses and refill the hay. When they finished the morning chores, they took Rascal and Winnie out to the ring to exercise them. Gemma took to the horses like she had been around them her whole life. The smile had not left her face since Becca first introduced her to Rascal and Winnie. Around noon, they put the horses back in their stalls, said their goodbyes and headed out.

"How about some lunch?" Becca asked as they put on their seat belts. They drove downtown to the Main Street Café. Conversation between the two of them never stopped flowing. Gemma asked if Becca would teach her how to ride. She also asked if she could come with her every Saturday to help out. By the time she dropped Gemma back at Claire's, they agreed, if it were okay with Claire and Patrick, Gemma could come and help at the stables on Saturday mornings in exchange Becca would teach her how to ride. The kid had great negotiation skills, Becca thought she'd make a great lawyer.

When they arrived at the house, Becca decided to walk Gemma up to the door so she could say hi to Claire and talk to her about the Saturday morning arrangement. As she approached the door, she realized this was the first time she had ever come to her sister's house that did not involve a family dinner or holiday. "Claire," she said as she cautiously walked through the front door behind Gemma.

"I'm back here. In the laundry room, " Claire yelled across the house. Becca walked through the living room, into the kitchen and around the corner to find Claire transferring laundry from one machine to the other. "Hey, how did today go?" Claire asked with her arms elbow deep in the top loading washer machine.

"Great. We had a fun time. Gemma took right to the horses. She's a natural with them. She asked me if she could come every Saturday morning to help out in exchange for riding lessons. I wanted to come in and see if you would be okay with it." Claire turned around to look at her sister.

"Really? That would be amazing, Becca. With the final play of the year wrapping up after spring break, I would love for her to have something else to do other than spend more time on technology. You don't mind?" Becca's heart caught in her throat. Mind, she would love it.

"Of course, not. If Grayson and Brita want to come sometime, they are welcome to as well." Becca was trying to keep her voice in control and not show off how happy she was to share her horses with Claire's kids.

"That would be amazing. Grayson still has soccer on the weekends, but once it's over, he'd love it. Brita is ecstatic about meeting Rascal and Winnie." Becca was taken aback. She didn't think her sister even knew the name of her horses. She looked around the laundry room. There were piles of clothes in baskets.

"I forgot how much laundry a family of five makes. It's been a long time since I had to help with laundry for that many people. Do you want some help folding?" The olive branch was being verbally passed between the two of them. "Unless it's weird to ask."

"Trust me, I'd rather have you folding our undergarments than Margie." They both laughed. "Patrick wasn't able to make it home again this weekend. They're having some issues that needed to be resolved by Monday. Looks like I am single parenting again. Please don't say anything negative about him though. I don't have it in me right now." Claire closed the washing machine and hit the start button.

"I wasn't going to say anything other than, I'm sorry for you." Becca picked up a laundry basket of clean clothes and carried them back toward the living room. Claire followed behind her with another basket which needed to be folded. They sat side-by-side on the couch folding the laundry and making the appropriate piles on the coffee table. It reminded Becca of when they were younger and had to do the same thing as part of their weekly chores.

"I don't hate Patrick," Becca said out of the blue. "Patrick and I, we haven't always gotten along."

She could tell her words threw Claire off. *Where did that come from?*

"That's for sure," Claire placed a folded sweatshirt on the growing pile in front of them.

"But I don't hate him. I think it's maybe because we both love you. Not in a competitive way. We want to protect you. When I moved home after law school, you were dating Patrick. I saw how serious you were. I was worried about you getting hurt. I still thought of you as my little Claire bear. It was hard for me to think of you as a grown woman with a boyfriend." Becca thought of the first time she visited their small apartment with her mother. That was the moment she realized she did not know this version of Claire at all, the grown woman.

"Becca, I'm not little anymore. You don't need to protect me. I'm not going to lie. I felt abandoned when you and Elana left for college. I was home all by myself with Mom and Dad. I was lonely without you two." Becca realized it was much easier for them to say these things when they were sitting side-by-side then having to look each other in the eyes. As hard as it was to say, she knew it was a conversation they needed to have.

"I had other boyfriends in high school and college, but Patrick was the only one who made me feel the unconditional love I was missing. Patrick filled the hole I needed filled in my heart. I'm also madly in love with the man. He's my partner. My soulmate. As corny as it may sound." Becca could sense the love Claire had for her husband. Something she admired and envied at the same time. Maybe one day she will have that too.

"I'm so sorry, Claire." Becca put down the shirt she was folding and turned to her sister. "I should have checked in on you more. When I left for college, I finally felt like I was living life for me. For so long, I had all of this responsibility on my shoulders. Going to college, I felt free. For once, I wasn't living under Mom's thumb. I'm sorry if you felt left behind."

Tears began to fall from Claire's eyes. "I was nine when you left and twelve when Laney left. I was lost and lonely without you guys. I had no one to talk to. When I needed to start wearing a training bra, Mom walked into my room and threw one of your old ones at me and said, start wearing this. That was it. That was my sex talk. When I got my period, I didn't even tell her until we ran out of pads, and I needed her to take me to the store to buy more. Her response was a sarcastic, welcome to womanhood."

Becca moved closer to Claire on the couch, putting an arm around her.

"I'm so sorry, Claire bear. I should have been there for you, to help you through that transition." It had been an extraordinarily long time since Becca called her by her childhood nickname. "I haven't been a good sister to you. I guess by the time I finished law school and moved back here you were already with Patrick and starting your future together. I was a little jealous."

"Jealous," Claire said in shock.

"Yes, jealous. I always wanted a family of my own. To be a wife, a mother. Instead, there I was following in Dad's footsteps, a lawyer, consumed by my work." Becca dropped her head and closed her eyes for a moment. Her internal feelings finally spoken.

"I didn't know you wanted a family. What about Frank? He wanted that too, didn't he?"

"Ugh...that was a disaster." She said sitting back up. "I never should have let Margie set me up with him. He was sweaty, hairy, messy, just gross. We had only been on one date, and he was already talking about marriage and kids. I went on a few more dates for Margie's sake, but that was it. It was horrible." Becca had a look of disgust on her face while recalling her dates with Frank.

Claire glanced over at her. Becca felt like Claire was starting to see the sister she knew growing up, not the masked one she'd turned into. "I am so sorry I've been so consumed with my own family I have neglected you. I want to do better."

"Claire, stop putting so much pressure on yourself to be the best for everybody. You're only human. We will never be able to make up for the loss of love we felt growing up. What we can do is try to love each other the best we can now."

"Wow, wise words from my big sister." They smiled at each other. "So, we start over."

"No, not over. No more resentment for the past. No more regret. Time to create a new sister friendship as adults." Becca placed the piles of folded laundry into the basket by her feet.

"Have you been talking to Mom?" Claire asked as she did the same with her stack of clothes in the basket on the floor next to her.

"Well, she is much easier to deal with in her old age. I don't mind her as much now that I have learned to say no and also I get to leave and go to my own house. Trust me, though, the unempathetic Justine is still in there. It's just easier to ignore her now." Becca was feeling so good by the time she left, she decided not to go home and do more work, but to head back to the stables and spend the rest of the day riding in the fields.

TWENTY-FOUR

Gemma could not stop talking about her morning at the farm. She had a permanent grin on her face since she got home. Patrick video chatted with them before dinner, Claire told him she couldn't remember the last time she had seen Gemma this excited about something. She even scooped horse poop and didn't complain about having done it. She then handed her cell phone over to Gemma so she could fill him in on her morning. After finishing her word vomiting, Gemma headed up to her room. She still needed to shower and change. She smelled like she brought the farm home with her.

Claire was back in the living room folding laundry with her cell phone propped up on the coffee table so she could keep folding while talking to him and seeing him on FaceTime. "Wow," he said. "This is an interesting turn of events."

"I know. Nothing I had expected at all. It's nice to see Becca and Gemma spending time together." She then filled him in on the conversation she had with Becca when they got back to the house.

Patrick looked at her through the phone with a half-smile. "So do you think you will start spending more time with your sister now too?"

She told him how Gemma kept saying Becca was misunderstood. She now understood what Gemma meant. Even though Patrick and Becca didn't always get along, he had a great relationship with his brother, and she knew he wanted the same for her with both of her sisters. "I don't know. Maybe I will."

***

As spring break approached, Claire felt she and the kids could use a change of scenery. Patrick couldn't get any time off from work. She decided to call Laney and see if she and the kids could visit her for a few days. Laney was ecstatic when she suggested it and began planning adventures for each day they would be there.

Thursday night before spring break, she got home from work with Brita and the house felt different. She couldn't quite figure out what it was. She walked through the living room into the kitchen and put her bags down. She looked around the room. *What's different?* She opened the fridge to grab a drink. She was almost blinded by the shine coming off of the shelves. The contents of the refrigerator had been moved around as well. Claire closed the door and walked the rooms in the house. It smelled like Clorox, Windex, Pine Sol and, she sniffed the air, Febreze. It smelled like a Walmart cleaning aisle. Her house had never been this clean. She slowly walked up the stairs and down the hall to the kids' bathroom. Their bathroom was spotless. The cap was on the toothpaste, there were no spit splatters on the mirror and the towels were folded and placed on the towel racks. She looked over at the roll of toilet paper and the end of it was folded into a nice, neat point with the ends tucked under.

She walked back down the stairs. Brita had her hand in a bag of Goldfish and there were crumbs all over the floor underneath her feet. *That didn't take long.* She grabbed her purse up from the floor, pulled out her cell phone and texted Patrick.

Did you hire a cleaning service?

No

Well, then the cleaning fairies must have been here because our house is too clean to be our house. There is no way your mom would have done all of this cleaning. Would she?

No, she probably hired someone to do it.

That took Claire back. She hadn't even thought about Margie hiring a cleaning service as a possibility.

I am not comfortable with your parents paying someone to clean our home.

I wouldn't make a big thing out of it. It was a nice thing for her to do.

I'm not going to make a big thing out of it. It would have been nice to be asked my thoughts on having the cleaning fairies in my house while I was away at work.

Just text her and say thank you.

Fine. I'll talk to you later.

She put her phone back down on the counter. There was an uncomfortable feeling back in her stomach. *Why is this irking me so much? Is it because I have a hard time receiving help from others or is it because she brought in the cleaning crew without talking to me first? Or is it because it's Margie and she knows how to get under my skin and make me feel worthless?* She picked her phone back up and found Margie's number and clicked on the message icon.

The house looks incredible. Thank you

You're welcome, dear. It was too much for you to keep up with and I can only do so much these days. So, I asked my girl to add you to their schedule. They will be there every other Thursday to clean. Don't worry about the expense, George and I got it. You're welcome.

Why was every conversation with her so passive/aggressive? Claire didn't even respond. She didn't feel comfortable having them pay for the house to be cleaned. She didn't feel comfortable with people being in her house every other week, especially since she's never met them. She decided to text her mom.

Margie has hired a cleaning crew to come into my house every other Thursday to clean.

Sounds about right.

Why does this bother me so much?

Because it's Margie.

Is that really why?

Probably. But Claire, it's okay. Let her.

She makes me feel incompetent and incapable of taking care of my own home.

Sounds like a you problem.

Thanks, Mom. She put her phone away and got out the hand vacuum to clean up the goldfish crumbs. Maybe they could keep the house clean for one night, or maybe one hour.

TWENTY-FIVE

Claire and the kids spent a restful week at Elana's house on the Cape. Elana owned a quaint little shop on Main Street in Orleans, Massachusetts. Everything they could want to do was either within walking or biking distance from her house. They spent their days walking on the beach, the nights grilling out and biking on the bike trail or going to get ice cream. There was still a nip in the air, as it was April, and they were by the ocean. The kids didn't seem to care that they couldn't swim in the ocean at all. They were so happy to be someplace different and spend time with their Aunt Laney. Claire was happy and relaxed as well. She didn't realize how tired she was after these past few months with Patrick's new work schedule, her job, and the kids.

It was Thursday night and their last night there; nobody wanted to leave but Patrick would be flying back, and Grayson had soccer games on Saturday and Sunday. The kids were in bed. Claire was sitting under a cozy blanket with a glass of white wine in her hand. Elana was across from her on the other couch doing the same thing. There were pillows and blankets smattered about on both couches. Elana's house oozed with the feeling of comfort. From its soothing color palette to its quant beachy accents.

"It's been so nice having you and the kids here this week," Laney said. Claire nodded her head in agreement while taking a sip of wine.

"I know. It is going to be hard to leave tomorrow," Claire closed her eyes, tilted her head back and savored the moment. She looked back over at Elana. "You would not believe Becca and Gemma. Gemma is like a different person since she started going to the stables with Becca. We might be past the terrible twelves."

"She has an outlet," Elana said.

"Well, she has theater club too," Claire pointed out.

"Yes, but this is something completely different for her. There are no grades, expectations, or anything tied to school or home. It's something that is hers. She's also sharing it with Becca." Claire had never thought about it like that. The stables and horses were her escape from her everyday life. She loved that for her daughter. She wondered if it was why Becca loved it so much as well. Probably.

"How about you?" Elana asked.

"How about me?" She was not sure she understood what her sister was asking her.

"What do you do for yourself? What's only yours?" Claire didn't know how to respond to her questions.

"I am the purpose person. I don't have time for anything just for me." Claire thought for a moment. "Even if I did, I wouldn't know what to do."

"Claire, you've been drowning yourself in your family for twelve years now. You need to have something that is your own. Take time to discover you, your interests, apart from your family. Maybe even try something new or something you've always wanted to do."

"Laney, I don't even know what I would do if I had time to myself. Probably take a nap." Claire smiled at the thought.

"Then take a nap. If that is what you do for yourself a couple of hours a week, do it? When Patrick is home on the weekends, tell him you are taking a couple of hours to yourself and go lie down." Claire shook her head. Her, lying down in her own house to sleep, undisturbed. She couldn't even imagine it. She decided to change the subject.

She took a sip of her wine, savoring the fruity flavor. "Let me ask your opinion about something. What are your thoughts about Margie hiring a cleaning service to clean my house every other week."

"Do you want my honest opinion? Never mind, I'm going to give it to you anyway. Patrick's mom likes control. She's been the only female in her house. She's used to being catered to and listened to. Her boys are grown and gone. She doesn't have much to do now that George is retired, and they are both at home. Joss is a force of nature and won't be pushed around by Margie. You're an easy target, so she came for you. You need to be stronger with her. Find your voice, Claire." Elana sealed her opinion with a big gulp of her wine.

"Wow, please don't hold back," Claire said sarcastically.

"The middle child is the most mature out of the siblings. I speak the truth." She laughed at herself. "All I'm saying is if you give her an inch, she'll take the inch, the foot, yard, mile, and anything else she feels she's entitled to. Claire, it's great the family is helping you out. You might want to set some boundaries."

Claire looked over at her. "That's easier said than done."

"It is," she said firmly. "Figure out what you're comfortable with, write it down and tell everyone at the next family dinner. Stop trying to people please. Find your voice, stand up for yourself. If you're not comfortable with something, say something."

Claire contemplated this for a second. "You make it sound so easy. I wish I were as comfortable in my own skin as you are."

"Well, it was easier for me growing up than you or Becca."

Claire looked over at her tilting her head to the side. "How so?"

"Being the middle sister, I was like the odd one out of the family. Becca was expected to be Mommy's little helper and you were expected to follow along and do what you were told. I kind of got lost in the mix, which was fine by me. As long as the three of us were together, I was good. I was able to do what I wanted as long as Mom's chore list got done. Most of the time, Mom and Dad didn't know what to do with me, so they left me alone. Of course, that was until I got pregnant with Danny. Then I was expected to get married and be a good little homemaker, which of course was not me. Thank God, Mark didn't expect that from me."

"I think Mom and Dad were more disappointed in you not finishing college than in you getting pregnant," Claire reminded her.

"College was never a place I wanted to go, but it was expected of us. Flannigan girls go to college," she said with a mocking shake of her head. "Dad had said when I mentioned the possibility of pursuing my art after high school that it was not an option. When I got pregnant in college and dropped out, I wasn't even sure they would talk to me again. Both sets of parents were not too happy with us, but at least Mark's parents were supportive."

Claire remembered it vividly. About a year after their son Danny was born, Mark and Elana moved to the Cape. Elana told her she couldn't be near their family anymore. College life wasn't for her, domestic life wasn't either. She couldn't stay in a place she knew would eat away at her soul. She needed freedom. Freedom to be her own person and raise her son. Being in their hometown felt suffocating. Claire knew she needed to find her community of like-minded artists. Mark finished his degree in architecture and found a job at a small company designing cookie cutter homes. He took on side jobs designing homes for people at a much better rate than they could get from hiring a firm. His employer found out about his side hustle, fired him, and he'd been working for himself ever since. He created a lucrative business for himself. Unfortunately, as his business grew, their marriage declined.

"Claire, you're stronger than you give yourself credit for. I set my boundaries by moving away. It was the best decision I made for my family. Mine and Mark's marriage didn't work out, but we are happily co-parenting Danny together, and I wouldn't change a thing about it." Claire looked over at her sister. She had always been impressed by Laney's fortitude. She needed more of that in her life too.

As she drove back to Connecticut the next morning, her conversation with Elana replayed over and over in her head. Her thoughts kept ruminating, and she couldn't get them to stop. She felt ungrateful for asking to change anything. She also knew she needed to start standing up for herself when it came to the extended family and also open herself up more to mending her relationships with them. Their next family dinner was two weeks away. She decided to put it out of her head for now and revisit it later. She also wanted to talk to Patrick. It had been too long since they'd had time to reconnect.

***

AS MAY APPROACHED, THE END OF THE SCHOOL YEAR ACTIVITIES began to take over their lives. Gemma had tech week followed by a weekend full of performances. Grayson's soccer season would be coming to an end with tournaments on Memorial Day weekend. Brita had her end of year celebration which Claire took a day off work to attend. Patrick had diagnostics happening in Chicago and would miss a few weekends at home. Her calendar was filling up quickly and the stress of the upcoming month was taking its toll on her before it was even there. She could feel her hair going gray in anticipation over the stress ahead of her.

They had their monthly family Sunday dinner on a weekend Patrick couldn't make it back. Claire's parents were hosting this one and her mom was a frantic mess to make sure everything was perfect.

Justine was running around from oven to refrigerator to countertop, mixing, mashing, and stirring. Claire was dizzy watching her. "Mom, can I please help with something?" Justine shook her head no and pushed her aside to get a seasoning out of the cabinet behind Claire's head. This kitchen was so small and cramped it could only fit three people at a time in it comfortably. Which was fine by her mom. She hated people in her kitchen.

"Go set the table," she barked at her.

"I already did," she snapped back.

"Did you use the cloth napkins?" Claire shook her head yes at her mother while picking at the salad on the counter. Justine slapped her hand away. "Then get out of my kitchen and talk to your family."

Claire pushed herself off the counter and headed into the living room. Joss, Greg, and the kids weren't there yet. They were running late. The fathers were watching a golf tournament. Her kids were on their technology. She decided to sit in the worn, floral armchair. "Margie how has your week been?" she asked, trying to think of something to talk about.

"Mine's been better than yours, I'm sure. With Patrick away, it must be hard. I mean he's working so hard; he's missing the kids, and you are home by yourself to manage it all. Thank goodness you have all of us to pick up the slack."

Claire didn't even know how to respond. Was it a back-handed compliment or an insult? "Luckily summer is around the corner, and I can focus on the kids," she said, putting a fake smile on her face. She was trying to keep the mood upbeat.

"That's true. I'm glad we can pay for the cleaners for you. I know it is impossible for you to keep up with the house and laundry while working." Claire patted Margie on her knee with a curt smile, stood up, and walked away. Little did Margie know Claire had called the cleaners and canceled them. She should probably have told her, but decided she'd rather not deal with it now. She couldn't get comfortable with strangers in her house while she was away or having her in-laws paying for it. She also didn't like being indebted to anyone, especially Margie.

Claire walked out the double French doors of the dining room to the back patio. She had been feeling very lonely lately with Patrick away for such long stretches of time. All the coordination on the outside for these new arrangements seemed to be falling in place, but Claire felt so empty. She felt like she was losing the emotional connection of her immediate family. She missed Patrick, she missed their time together snuggling up on the couch or laughing together in bed. She missed the way he would move her hair off of her neck and kiss her while handing her a cup of coffee in the morning and the way he would reach over to hold her hand while he was driving. Just thinking about it made her heartsick for him. She understood it took a village, but why did her village seem to be coming at her with pitchforks and torches? Her husband was halfway across the country. She felt completely disconnected from him. Her family was helping out more and she should be grateful, instead, she felt like a moveable piece in her own life. Her life was a game of chess and she's the pawn only able to move forward. No say in what's happening with the other pieces around her. She tilted her head up to the sky to take in a little bit of sunlight. She swallowed the lump forming in her throat and cleared the tears forming in the corners of her eyes. Time to put on a smile and pretend all was okay. She knew she had promised Laney she would talk to the family and set some boundaries. She was feeling too vulnerable and couldn't bring herself to do it that day. She needed Patrick by her side. She decided to put it off, again, for another time. She turned around and headed back into her parents' house.

That night Patrick called and spent time talking to each kid. They were all very animated to tell him about everything going on in their world. When Grayson brought her cell phone to her, she tried to sound happier than she felt. He could tell right away something was wrong. "Babe, are you okay?"

That was all he had to say for the tears to start falling. "It's all caving in on me."

"What do you want me to do?" She could hear sadness in his voice. She knew he felt bad for the position he had put her in. "What can I do?" His tone switched to frustration.

"Nothing. I need you to hear me." Claire wiped away at the tears forming at the corners of her eyes.

"I do. I hear you, Claire, and I'm so sorry. Are you regretting me taking the job?" She wanted to say yes, but she didn't want to make him feel bad.

"No, it's not that. I'm glad we don't have money worries anymore. I'm so proud of you. I know it's not easy for you either flying back and forth each week, missing the kids and being at their activities. I'm...I'm having a moment. I'll be okay."

"Are you sure?" He said it so lovingly it ripped at her heart.

"Yeah. I'm sorry. I'm really tired. I think I need to go to bed." Her lip started to quiver. She knew she needed to get off the phone with him before she started to ugly cry.

"Okay," he said. "I understand. I'll let you go. Love you," he said with resignation.

"Love you too." As Claire hung up the phone, she realized this was the first time she had lied to Patrick. She wished he hadn't taken the job. She missed him. She missed them. She needed him. The kids needed him. She wanted him next to her when she fell asleep at night and there when she woke up. She would rather have pinched pennies than keep living this way. She knew it was only for one year and they were almost halfway there, but she couldn't stop how she was feeling in that moment. The plates weren't spinning anymore. They were crashing down around her. The stress of the past months were finally catching up to her.

TWENTY-SIX

Claire's father-in-law had started helping Joss and Greg with carpooling their two kids now that Joss's due date was getting closer. Claire's mother was the only grandparent not helping out with the grandkids, but that's exactly how she'd always been. Justine delegated, observed, and then would show up at the end to criticize what hadn't been done or act like the hero saving the day. It had become a bit of a contention between Claire and Patrick with him not able to make it home on some of the weekends. They were both under a lot of stress and started taking it out on each other.

This back-and-forth defensive arguing seemed to be the only way Patrick and Claire conversed these days. There had been so much tension between them on their phone calls when talking about it. This happened the last time he was unable to come home for the weekend. There was too much distance between them. They were good after their weekends together as a family and then a gap in time and the fighting about family issues started. They barely had time to talk each day and then they end up arguing, irritated with each other and the whole situation. The last time they spoke Patrick complained to her about the lack of support from Justine. Claire hung up the phone and tossed it down on her comforter. Thinking about what Patrick said, she decided to text her mom.

Hey mom, would you and dad be able to take the kids next Friday night so Patrick and I can have a date night.

Sure, we'd love to.

Thank you, we really appreciate it.

Anytime.

Claire wanted to respond with "then why haven't you," but she knew it was her own irritation from her conversation with Patrick that would be responding.

Thank you

Claire could hear Gemma still moving in her room and decided to have a check-in with her. She threw the covers off of herself and headed down to her room. She gently knocked on the door and peeked her head in. "Hey sweets, do you mind if I come in for a second?" Gemma was sitting up in her bed reading a book with the gentle glow of her flower lamp shining from the nightstand.

"Sure. What's up?"

"Not much. I just wanted to check-in with you. See how you are, how school is, how the play is coming along? I feel like we don't have one-on-one time anymore." Gemma placed her bookmark in her book and then set her book down on her lap.

"Everything's good. School is school, sets are done for the show, and we are almost done with all of the blocking with them. Yeah, not much else."

"And how about Saturdays with Aunt Becca?" She had barely finished the sentence when Gemma jumped in.

"Oh my God, Mom. They are so great. I love the horses. Winnie is the sweetest, and Rascal lives up to her name. If I have any treats in my pockets, she'll sniff them out and try digging them out with her nose. She is so funny. Aunt Becca lets me exercise them and this week she started teaching me how to care for their saddles and even put them on. Winnie's is easier to get on her. Rascal thinks she's going riding and gets so excited it's hard to keep her still to get her saddle on," she said laughing. "Aunt Becca said once I have mastered the care of them and understanding of their equipment, she'll start teaching me how to ride."

"Wow, Gemma, that's fantastic. I haven't seen you this excited over anything in a long time." Claire was happy for her and a little envious of Becca that she got to share this newfound love with her daughter.

"I really am. I absolutely love being at the stables. I can't believe it took me so long to learn Aunt Becca had horses and how much she loves to ride. Do you know she goes to the stables almost every morning at five a.m. before work? Also, sometimes she goes after work and will take one of them out for a ride to decompress from the day? Isn't that so cool? I want to be able to do that too. When I'm older and driving, I want to get out of school and go riding. It sounds so freeing, doesn't it?" Claire smiled at her. It was so nice to see this much enthusiasm oozing from her daughter. She gave her a kiss on the forehead, said goodnight, and slowly closed the bedroom door behind her. She's so glad her inner turmoil wasn't affecting her daughter. She's incredibly grateful to Becca for it.

She stopped in Grayson's room next. She peeked in the door expecting him to be sound asleep. Instead, she found him on his iPad. "Hey bud, what are you doing? It's late. You should be asleep."

"I'm texting with Dad, filling him in on my games from this weekend." He looked up over at her from his device.

"You miss him, don't you?" she said with a pained expression.

He gave her a half smile and shook his head yes. Her sweet boy was lying under his favorite navy-blue blanket. She hoped he never gave it up. It was all stretched out in one corner where he used to suck on it when he was little. "Well, I think next weekend, when he is home, the two of you should have a father-son day. Lake Compounce is open on the weekends now. You could hit all of your favorite roller coasters together."

"Really? That would be awesome! I'm going to text him about it right now."

"Okay, then after that, sleep." She walked out of his room and back to her own bed. There was something about seeing her children happy that made all her own issues seem much less important.

Claire woke up the following Monday morning and then blinked and it was Friday afternoon. She couldn't remember what she ate, if she slept, or how she functioned through the days. She was so excited and nervous for Patrick to get home. They texted more than talked throughout the week. There was still some tension from their previous phone conversation. It was easier to text updates on how the days went.

Claire picked up Brita from daycare and was home by four-fifteen. It felt great to be home. They walked in the door and Patrick was sitting in the living room with the older kids, relaxing and spending time with them. She got butterflies in her stomach from seeing him sitting there. He stood up, walked over, and gave her the biggest hug. She melted into his arms. That's all she needed from him, that's all she ever needed from him, reassurance. It's all going to be okay.

They spent some time together as a family and then got the kids packed up for their sleepover at her parents' house. "Well, look who cleans up nicely," Joe said as he opened the door for them. Claire and Patrick were both dressed up for their special date night.

"Memes, Memes, I'm here," Brita said as she dropped her overnight bag on the floor and ran through the house looking for Justine. They all laughed, and Claire gave her dad a hug.

"Thanks again for having them, Dad." Her dad was shocked at first and then hugged her back. They had never been a touchy-feely family. It felt good to hug her dad.

"Yeah, thanks, Joe. We appreciate it." Joe and Patrick shook hands. Joe patted Patrick on the back.

"Of course, we love having them all to ourselves. Trust me, Memes has tons of activities planned and we will send them home tomorrow all sugared up for you." He chuckled at his own joke. Justine walked into the living room with a strange substance in her hands.

"Is that slime?" Claire asked, completely dumbfounded.

"It sure is," she said, smiling mischievously at her.

"Oh Mom, you don't know what you are getting yourself into," she told her.

"I sure do. The stain is still on my kitchen ceiling from Elana. We're going to make a few different batches together. Maybe we'll add more colors up there. It's going to be so fun," she said laughing as she turned and walked away. "Have fun tonight!"

Patrick and Claire walked around the house and said goodbye to the kids who were dispersed in various rooms. After they finally got into the car and put their seatbelts on, they turned and looked at each other.

"Hi," he said.

"Hi," she said back. Claire was hoping all the tension from the last couple of weeks would melt away and they could spend the rest of the evening and night reconnecting with each other.

Unfortunately, that was not what happened. They drove to their favorite restaurant. When the host asked them what name the reservation was under, Claire realized she forgot to call and make one. It was a ninety-minute wait for a table and the bar was packed. She could tell Patrick was a bit annoyed and she wanted to tell him he could have made the reservation himself, but she didn't want to start an argument with him. They left and drove around town naming different restaurants they could go to. Being it was a Friday night, most of the restaurants were packed with people. They decided to pick up take out from a local Thai restaurant and bring it home. Once home, they changed out of their fancy attire into their comfy clothes, set up their chicken Pad Thai and shrimp spring rolls on plates and brought them into the living room.

Claire turned on the television and cued up Netflix. She looked over at her husband as he took the first bite from his chopsticks. *This is kind of nice. The two of us...having a quiet night at home.* She poured them both wine from the bottle on the coffee table, thinking to herself this could lead to the reconnection they both need so badly. It felt like it had been months since they had any alone time or anytime to be intimate with each other.

Four hours later, Claire woke up on the couch covered in a blanket. She looked over to the other side and didn't see Patrick there. She realized she fell asleep while watching the movie. She pulled herself off the couch and looked around. Patrick had cleaned up their dinner dishes already. Claire walked up the stairs to their bedroom and found Patrick breathing heavily, sound asleep. So much for intimacy.

She climbed into bed next to him hoping to arouse him a little. When he didn't move, she rolled over to her side of the bed and fell back to sleep with sadness in her heart.

***

THE NEXT MORNING, CLAIRE DROVE OVER TO PICK UP GEMMA and Brita. Patrick was meeting her father at soccer to watch Grayson's game. After the game, the boys were heading to Lake Compounce for a guy's day together.

"Thanks for having the kids over last night," Claire said, sitting at the kitchen table with a cup of coffee.

"We love having the kids over. You can ask us anytime."

"Honestly? Then why don't you ever ask to have them sleep over, Mom." She blew on her coffee not looking at her mother.

"You never ask us to. We figured you'd let us know if you needed us. Again, Claire, all you have to do is ask."

She didn't respond. She sat there thinking about what Patrick said about the difference between both of their mothers. Her mom didn't offer, she assumed they knew she was there if they needed her. While Patrick's mom was incessantly offering her advice or telling them what to do. Claire was realizing she needed to find balance in her life with

ALL of her family. She was feeling closer to her sisters but now she felt distance from her husband and needed to come to terms with her relationships with the mothers.

The weekend finished with a blur and Patrick had to leave early Monday morning again. They were both too distracted with the kids and the to-do list that they did not get a chance to talk themselves or have any one-on-one time before he left. Patrick was getting ready when Claire's eyes fluttered open.

"Hey," she said.

"Hey."

"Patrick, something's not right with us."

"I know."

"I don't like it."

"Me either."

"Can we please try again next weekend? I feel like we're business partners more than spouses."

Patrick walked over to her and sat on the edge of the bed with a sad look on his face. "Babe, I'm so sorry. I won't be able to make it home next weekend. There's too much going on."

"What? But next weekend is everything. Gemma's play, Grayson's soccer games, Brita, me." Claire could feel irritation rising up in herself.

"I've already talked to the kids. You knew this month was going to be crazy and I wouldn't be able to come home every weekend. I am so sorry."

She could tell he really was sorry; it was not making the hurt feeling in her heart feel any better.

Sadness and anger flared up in Claire's eyes. "I am so sick of you saying you're sorry. I'm drowning over here, Patrick. I want my husband back. I don't like this anymore."

Patrick's voice began to rise to meet hers. "What do you want me to do? We both agreed to me taking this job. There's only six months left of this contract. Summer is here soon, and you'll be home with the kids. You have to suck it up for a few more weeks."

"Suck it up!" Fire was flaring up inside her.

"That's not what I meant." He stood up and ran his fingers through his auburn hair in frustration.

"You know what, go. Go before either of us say anything else we are going to regret." She turned her back on him and buried herself into her pillow.

"Fine," he said, sighing dejectedly. "I'll call you tonight." She wanted to say *don't bother* but she knew it would be coming from a place of anger.

Patrick walked out of their bedroom. She listened as he walked down the stairs and to the garage. A part of her wanted him to come back. She wanted him to crawl into bed with her, hold her and tell her it would all be okay. That same feeling of abandonment began to creep in that she had when Becca and Laney left for college. "Mom?" She heard Gemma's voice on the other side of her door. "Mom, are you okay?"

"Yeah, honey. I'm okay. Dad and I had a cranky morning fight. We're fine. I'm going to get up now and make coffee." She heard Gemma's feet pad back down the hallway to her room. Gemma normally was a sound sleeper; of all days for her to decide to be a light sleeper, it was to hear her parents arguing.

TWENTY-SEVEN

Wednesday night, Gemma ran into the house slammed the door and raced up the stairs to her bedroom, slamming that door as well. Claire walked into the living room from the kitchen as Becca came into the house.

"What was that all about?" Claire turned to her sister while drying her hands on the dish towel she was holding.

Becca closed the door behind her. Claire could see the worry in her eyes. "While Gemma was waiting for me, she overheard some of the moms talking after rehearsal. It wasn't great, Claire. When I pulled up, she ran to my car, jumped in, and slammed the door saying some words I don't think I should repeat."

Claire couldn't imagine what the school moms could have said to upset Gemma so badly. She normally tuned out the mom talk. "What were they saying?"

"I didn't get the full story, but it had to do with Patrick and the 500-mile rule. I'm so sorry." Becca walked over and placed her hand on Claire's arm.

"What's the 500-mile rule?" Claire naively asked.

Claire could see Becca was uncomfortable with whatever she was about to tell her by the way she wasn't make eye contact with her, "The 500-mile rule means when someone is five hundred miles or more from their home without their husband or wife, they can't be held accountable for their actions. It's basically permission to cheat."

Claire stared at her sister in shock. "What? Are you freaking kidding me? Stupid ass people need to mind their own damn business. Poor Gemma. She should know her father better than that."

"I really don't want to say the next part but feel you should know everything Gemma told me," Becca cleared her throat. "She also heard them say you would probably end up divorced by the end of the year."

"And of course, the last conversation she heard us have was an argument. Oh, my poor girl." Claire turned and looked up the stairs. "Becca, do you mind? I'm going to go talk to her."

"Oh, my goodness, of course not. I wanted to come in and tell you what was going on." Claire walked over to Becca and gave her a hug and thanked her.

She threw the dish towel into the kitchen not caring where it landed, then headed up the stairs and down the hall to Gemma's room. She quietly knocked and opened the door. Gemma was lying across her bed crying. "Gem, hon, can we talk?"

"Are you and Dad getting divorced?" she mumbled with her face smushed into her pillow.

"Of course not." Claire sat down at the head of Becca's bed, leaned against the headboard, and pulled her daughter to her. "Aunt Becca told me what you overheard those moms saying. I am so, so sorry, honey."

"Stupid ass bitches." Gemma curled herself up into a fetal position next to Claire resting her head in the crook of her mother's shoulder. Claire didn't correct her language.

"You're right. They *are* stupid ass bitches. They have no right to talk about or judge our family." Claire smoothed Gemma's hair away from her face. Anger rose in Claire, but she contained it for her daughter's sake.

"Is Dad cheating on you?" Her sad face stared up at Claire. Tears streaked down her cheeks.

"No, never. Dad loves us all very much and would never, ever do anything like that." Claire gently smoothed Gemma's hair with her hand like she did when the kids were sick to comfort her.

"Why does he have to be away? Why did he have to take this job? I hate it. I want him home with us." Her voice sounded so small to Claire.

"Me too, sweetie. There's only six more months left and then he'll be home."

It took Claire an hour to calm Gemma down and reassure her their marriage was fine, their family was fine. At some point, Brita and Grayson came into their sister's room to see what was going on.

"Why is Gemma sad?" Brita asked, sucking on her favorite bunny's ear.

"She misses Dad." Claire pulled Brita onto the bed next to Gemma while Grayson sat down at the end.

"I miss Daddy, too," she said snuggling up to her sister.

Grayson reached over and tugged at her bunny. "We all do."

"I'm so sorry you guys. I know these last few months have been crazy. Dad's contract is only for a year and he's halfway through it. He'll be home with us before you know it."

"Will he be home this weekend?" Gemma looked up at Claire with her big, blue eyes, Patrick's eyes. It broke Claire's heart. She could see her little baby girl staring up at her wanting to know when her daddy would be home from work.

"Gemma, he can't make it home this weekend. I am so, so sorry. In fact, he won't be home much this month. It's a super busy month for him at the other office."

"He's going to miss my play." Gemma began crying again. Brita leaned over and handed Gemma her bunny with the soggy ear.

"Will he be home for my soccer tournament?" Grayson stared at her waiting for her response. She could tell he was trying to hold back tears as well.

"I don't know, Gray. We'll have to ask him when he calls." A tear slid down from Grayson's eye. She knew how much they all missed their father. They had been such troopers with all of the changes. Claire wished she could do something to comfort them.

"Let's call him. It will make us all feel better." She pulled her cell phone out of her back pocket. She clicked Patrick's name in her phone's favorites menu. It rang five times and went to voicemail. "Hi babe," she said in a tone more cheerful than she felt. "Here with the kids. We were hoping to chat with you. Call us back when you can. We love you. Bye."

She ended the call and pulled all three kids into a big family hug. "Brita, will you go to your room and get Mama a book. I think tonight is a good night for a bedtime story for all of us." Brita looked up at her mother with a big smile on her face, then jumped down from the bed and ran to her room. A few minutes later she came running back in with the book *Knuffle Bunny*. She curled herself in between Grayson and Gemma with her bunny and Claire read her children a bedtime story, something she hadn't done in a while.

TWENTY-EIGHT

After Claire put all three kids to bed individually and made sure they each had some special time with her, she walked downstairs and into the kitchen. She was emotionally drained. She needed Patrick to have picked up the phone when she called him with the kids. She needed to hear his voice. She needed him to reassure their children they are a complete family, a loving family.

She decided to make herself a cup of tea. Standing at the counter waiting for the water to warm up in the microwave a memory flashed into her mind.

She was sixteen and had finished her driver's education class for the day. She was outside of her high school waiting for her mother to pick her up. She watched as the other kids from her class slowly dispersed into their parent's cars. She kept looking down toward the entrance of the school for her mom's car. Three different cars pulled into the lot, none of them were for her. "Claire, do you need a ride home?" Her friend, Emily's mom, leaned over Emily and yelled out the passenger side window.

"No, thank you, Mrs. Sordino. My mom should be here any minute." The woman waved to her and drove off in the stream of cars. Claire watched as everyone left. She was the last one standing at the front doors of her school. Twenty minutes slowly passed by, and her mother still had not shown up.

"Claire," Mr. Gianni, the school principal, stood at the front door holding it open with one hand. "Do you want to come in and call someone?"

"Sure, that would be great. Thank you." She had been biting her nails and now her thumbnail hurt from chewing it too low. She followed him into the main office. The office was empty. The staff had already left for the day. He walked over to the secretary's desk and turned the office phone toward her. She picked up the receiver and dialed her home telephone number. Her mother answered on the third ring.

"Hello." She sounded out of breath.

"Hi Mom." Claire covered the speaker phone with her hand so Mr. Gianni couldn't hear her talking.

"Claire, where are you? I thought I'd get home, and you would have had dinner started." Her mom sounded upset with her.

"I had driver's ed after school today. You were supposed to pick me up." Claire waited during a few beats of silence.

"Oh right, right. Well, I can't pick you up, because now I have to start dinner. You'll have to walk home."

Claire turned away from her principal as she didn't want him to see the tears welling up in her eyes. "You want me to walk home?" she whispered into the phone.

"It's only about three miles. The fresh air will be good for you. I have to go start dinner. I'll see you when you get here." Claire heard the click of the phone as her mother hung up.

"Everything okay?" Mr. Gianni asked.

She hung up the receiver but would not make eye contact with her principal. "Yeah, I'm going to walk home. It's not far. Thank you for letting me use the phone."

"I'm sorry, Claire. I'd offer to give you a ride but it's against school policy." He walked over to the desk and turned the telephone back around.

"It's fine, really. It's not that far. Thank you." Claire turned and walked out of the office and out the school's front door. It took her fifty minutes to walk home. Most of it she spent silently crying.

***

THE IMAGES FROM THIS MEMORY WASHED OVER HER. THE EMOtions from the night brought up the same feeling of abandonment. She thought Patrick was finally the one person who would never cast her aside. Deep, pent-up emotions, along with exhaustion, overcame her. She forgot about her tea in the microwave and ran into the laundry closet. Closing the tri-fold doors she sank down to the floor, and guttural cried into a piece of dirty laundry from the pile in front of her.

Why is everyone always leaving me? What's wrong with me? Why don't they love me enough to stay?

She kept repeating this over and over in her head until she eventually cried herself out of tears and rested her head on the washing machine.

"Mom," she heard Gemma's voice whisper and a quiet tap on the door. She did not want her daughter to see her this way.

"Claire?" She heard another voice. She glanced upward as the door slowly opened. Becca was standing there with Gemma slightly behind her. "Hey, sis." Becca knelt down next to her and pulled her into her arms. Claire melted into her big sisters' arms like she had done so many times before when they were younger.

"What are you doing here?" Claire asked in a hoarse voice.

Becca pulled away from the hug and looked up at her niece with loving eyes. "I called Gemma to check on her and then asked her if I could talk to you. She came down to give you the phone and heard you crying. She asked me to come over."

Claire looked up at her daughter. "Oh honey, I'm so sorry if I scared you."

"You didn't scare me, Mom. I'm worried about you. Are you okay?" She looked at her mother like one would look at a wounded animal.

"Yeah, I'm okay. I was feeling sad. I needed to cry it out. I'm okay now. You should head up to bed." She held her arms open to her daughter who bent down and hugged her mother tightly. Claire could tell Gemma wasn't convinced she was okay but left anyway. They watched Gemma leave the kitchen and then Becca pulled Claire back into her arms.

"I am so sorry you are hurting." Becca righted herself so she was sitting next to Claire and leaning on the washer machine.

"Why does everyone keep leaving me?" she whimpered. "What's wrong with me? Why doesn't anyone stay?" She cried into her sister's shoulder.

"Oh, Claire." Claire held onto her sister and let go of years of sadness. Sadness for the little girl she once was. Sadness for how she was feeling now.

"Come on. Let me help you up and I'll make us some tea." Becca helped Claire up off the floor and over to the kitchen table.

"I had started heating up some water..." Claire was too drained to even finish the sentence. Becca found the mug in the microwave and reheated it. She grabbed another one out of the cabinet for herself and then got out the tea bags. Once the tea was made, she handed her sister one of the mugs and sat down across from her.

She patted Claire on the hand. "We can talk, I can listen, or we can sit in silence. Whatever you need."

Claire looked up at her big sister and softly said, "Flannigan girls stick together." Becca smiled at her.

"Yes, Flannigan girls stick together."

"When I became a mother, I swore to myself I was not going to be like Mom. I would always be there for my children. They would always feel loved by me, by us. We'd be a family that stuck together and now it's all falling apart." Tears began to fall again.

"You have that. You are that and more. You don't have to be everything to everybody all the time. Your children don't expect it. You are putting too much pressure on yourself to not be like mom. Just be you. Loving, caring Claire with a big heart. You do not need to people please anymore. Give yourself some grace. Give yourself credit for the great family you do have. That you and Patrick have built together." Becca was saying all the words Claire needed to hear, she also needed to start believing them as well.

Claire and Becca eventually moved to the living room talking late into the night. They caught up on years of missed conversations. She learned about her sister's pro bono work and her dating history. When the kids woke up the next morning. They found their mother and aunt sleeping side by side on the couch. Brita woke them both up. They were all going to be late that morning and Claire didn't even care. Brita climbed onto the couch in between the two sisters. "Aunt Becca, Mama said you have horses."

Becca sat up from her side of the couch and looked down at her niece. "Yes, Brita. I have two horses who I love very much. You can meet them sometime if you want to."

"Wahoo" she said excitedly. "I guess if you love horses then you're not a grumpy bird." Becca looked up at Claire for an explanation. Claire shrugged her shoulders.

Gemma and Grayson came down next. Gemma gave them both a half smile and then headed out to catch the bus. Claire could tell she was still upset. She wasn't sure if it was about Patrick missing her play that weekend or what those nasty school moms said, probably a combination of both. "Hey, Aunt Becca," Grayson said, plopping down in the chair next to them.

"Morning Grayson. Do you want a ride to school today?" Becca asked him.

Grayson looked over at her in his casual way. "Nah, I'm good. I can catch the bus. Maybe another time."

"I want a ride to school today?" Brita chirped. "You can meet my school friends."

"I would love it. If it's okay with your mom." Claire gave a nod.

"If you want Aunt Becca to meet your school friends you better run upstairs and get yourself dressed." Brita gave her mother a big hug and then raced up the stairs with her bedhead of brown hair flapping in the air with each step.

"Claire, you don't have to worry about your family being anything like ours. You ooze love for those three kids, and they ooze it right back to you." Becca patted her on the arm.

"And my marriage?" Claire asked.

"Your marriage will be fine. These are the ebbs and flows of life. Remember, you can't make it perfect. Life is not perfect." Claire reached over and pulled her sister into a hug. She rose from the couch to get herself ready for work.

***

BECCA HAD NO IDEA HOW MUCH WENT INTO INSTALLING A child's car seat. Claire and Becca got so frustrated with trying to install it into Becca's Range Rover they decided to switch cars for the day.

Claire felt like a badass driving to work in the sleek vehicle. So much better than the minivan. She got to school at the same time as Greta. "Well, well. What do we have here? A bit of an upgrade I would think." Greta walked around the car while Claire gathered all her school bags.

"It's Becca's. We switched cars today so she could take Brita to day-care. If I'm being honest, I would have no problem with her not asking for it back." Claire was grinning from ear to ear.

"Becca's, huh? Looked like we have a lot of catching up to do today." They walked side by side toward the building.

"Greta, you have no idea. Since I saw you yesterday, I have been on the biggest emotional roller coaster of my life." Claire used her key card to let them into the building.

"I'll grab the chocolate and meet you in your room. I might need the abridged version until lunch." Although she was still feeling unsettled about what happened with Gemma last night, Claire was at least feeling a bit better after talking things through with her sister. It will be good to fill Elana in on everything too.

TWENTY-NINE

Becca had so much fun dropping Brita off at daycare. She discovered her little niece was quite the hot ticket. When they got to daycare, Brita led her all around her classroom. She introduced her to all her teachers and her friends. She told them all she owned two horses and was not a grump. After the introductions, Brita showed her all the different centers in the room.

"That's the kitchen. That's where I play the most. I get to be Mama there and make dinner for everyone like Mama does." She grabbed Becca's hand and dragged her over to another center where an art project was taking place. "We do art here every day. I like to play here the most too. Sit here you can make one and hang it on your refrigerator at home." Brita handed Becca a piece of yellow construction paper, a glue stick, and a pile of tissue paper squares.

Becca had a permanent smile on her face while they did their art projects together. Afterward, she said goodbye to Brita and told her she would see her at pick-up. When she walked out to the car, she decided to text Elana.

I think I'm going to fly Claire out to see Patrick this weekend.

Do it!

Is it overstepping?

Probably. Text Patrick.

Awkward.

Olive branch.

Okay.

Do you have his number?

No, can you send it to me?

Becca's phone pinged with an incoming message. It was Patrick's contact information from Elana. Becca didn't know where to begin. She decided to call him instead of sending a text as there was too much to put in a text message.

"Patrick Rhodes speaking," he said after two rings.

"Hi Patrick, it's Becca." She didn't sound as confident as she had hoped she would.

"Becca, oh my god, are the kids, okay? Is Claire, okay?" His voice changed from his business tone to one of panic.

"Yes, yes, I'm sorry. I didn't mean to worry you. They are all fine. Well, let me take that back. They are all physically fine. Emotionally, not so much." Becca filled Patrick in on the conversation Gemma overheard and the emotional breakdown Claire had after the kids went to bed. She shared with him her idea of flying Claire out to see him.

"I hate all those busy body moms. They have nothing else to do but gossip about other people's lives. Poor Gem, I feel so bad for her. I know Claire and I need more time together. I've been feeling it too. There has been such a strain between us lately." Becca could tell he was thinking out loud more than talking to her. "We are not the kind of couple who like to be apart. We really like each other's company. But who would stay with the kids?"

"I could stay with the kids," she said.

"Wow, that's very generous of you, Becca. I appreciate your offer. Gemma has her school play this weekend though. I doubt Claire would leave her." Becca could hear him shuffling through papers on the other end of the phone.

"I could also be there at Gemma's school play." She would actually enjoy going to Gemma's play since hearing all about it on their rides together.

"Let me figure out my schedule. Can I call you back in about fifteen minutes?" Becca could tell his mind was turning. She agreed to chat with him in a bit.

While she waited for his call, she walked over to her desk and opened her laptop. She sat down and began searching for airline tickets. They actually weren't as expensive as Becca expected them to be. *Claire could fly out tonight and stay through Monday night. It would give her three days with Patrick. She would need to call out of work for one day.* As she continued to scan other flight options, her phone rang. It was Patrick.

"Hello." She rested the phone on her shoulder, while continuing to scroll.

"I'm coming home." Becca pulled herself upright at her desk.

"Really?"

"Yes, I told my supervisor we had a family emergency and I needed to fly home. I'll be there later this afternoon."

"Oh, Patrick. Thank you. Claire and the kids are going to be so happy. They all need you." Becca couldn't hold back her excitement for her little sister.

"Thank you for calling, Becca. I really appreciate it." She was a bit taken aback.

"You're welcome." Had they taken a turn in their relationship, Becca wondered. This was the first halfway decent conversation the two of them had ever had. Becca hung up the phone and immediately texted Elana.

Patrick is flying home.

Did you threaten him?

No. LOL. He told work he had a family emergency and has to fly home.

He's not such a bad guy after all. Is he?

He loves her as much as we do.

Yes, he does.

THIRTY

Gemma's play started at seven on Friday night. It gave Claire enough time to get home and feed everyone and get to the school on time for the show. She decided to keep things easy by picking up pizza on her way home from work. As she walked through the front door, she heard voices coming from the kitchen. Brita ran ahead of her, almost knocking the pizza out of her hand. "Whoa. Sweet pea, be careful." She dropped the bags off of her shoulder onto the floor and walked into the kitchen.

Her face dropped in shock when she saw Patrick standing at the kitchen island with Gemma and Grayson. The three of them were eating pizza. "What? What? How? You're here?" Patrick walked around the island. He took the pizza out of her hand and placed it on the counter.

"Yeah, I'm here," he said softly, pulling her into a hug. She was so stunned it took her a minute before she wrapped her arms around him, squeezing him in tight.

"I don't understand. I thought you said you couldn't make it this weekend." She rested her head on his chest. She felt like she could finally breathe. The comfort of him was everything to her. He was home. He was her home.

"Becca called me. She told me about everything that happened last night. She was even going to fly you out to see me. I decided I needed to be here with my family. See you, see the play Gemma's been working so hard on, see Grayson's games and spend time with Brita." He looked around at each family member as he said their names.

"Becca called you? On the phone?" She was having a tough time forming complete sentences.

"Yes, she called me on the phone." It finally dawned on Claire he was actually there, in person. She hugged him tighter wishing she could hold onto him like this forever. A wave of love for her husband rushed over her. "You're here to be with your family." The little girl in her felt her heart expand with unconditional love.

"Yes, babe. I'm here. You are all more important to me than anything else in the world, money, or job." Claire started to cry, of course, but these were happy tears.

"Mama cries a lot, Daddy." They all laughed at Brita's candid observation.

"Yes, but I think this time it's because she's so happy to have the five of us together." He bent down, kissed her on the lips, and pulled her back into him.

"You're here," she whispered into his shoulder.

"I'm here. I will never abandon you." She knew that he knew how much those words meant to her. "Well," he turned to the kids. "Looks like we have a lot of pizza to eat before I drive Gemma over for her call time." They all laughed as he scooped Brita up onto his hip and carried her and one of the boxes of pizza over to the kitchen table. The rest of them followed him over bringing plates, napkins, and the other pizza. Claire looked around the table at her family, back together.

***

THEY ALL ATTENDED GEMMA'S PLAY. THE GIRL WHO PLAYED PETER Pan did a phenomenal job and Captain Hook had the audience laughing with his antics. Brita fell asleep on the ride home. Patrick and Claire stayed up late curled up on the couch next to each other catching up on life, and talking about ways to make the next six months work better for all of them. Even having she and the kids fly out to see him now and then. Eventually, they made their way up to their bedroom hand in hand. They had reconnected emotionally know it was time for them to reconnect physically. She couldn't wait to feel him next to her. Time and distance fused together in the intimacy of their love.

Saturday was a super busy day, but Claire would never complain. It was the kind of busy she thrived on. Being with her family and running the kids to all of their activities, playing with Brita and Patrick in the backyard. The house was a mess, the laundry needed to be done and Claire didn't care. The purpose person was taking a day off to enjoy her family time.

Sunday's matinee was the last performance of the show. The whole extended family was meeting at the school to see the show and then going back to Claire and Patrick's for family dinner. In their family group text, they all agreed take-out for dinner would be the easiest. Claire loved the idea as it was less for her to do. When Claire and Patrick pulled into the parking lot at the middle school, she saw her parents standing by their car with Becca and someone else.

"Is that Elana?" she asked, as she squinted through the sun shining into the windshield.

"It is, it is. It's Auntie Laney!" Brita exclaimed, bouncing up and down in her car seat. Patrick pulled into the first spot he could find. The four Flannigan's walked over to their minivan. Claire opened the door.

"Laney, what are you doing here?" Claire jumped out of the car and gave her sister a giant hug.

"You don't think I would miss my niece's play, do you?" Elana said while returning the hug.

"Wow, I can't believe you are here. You're all here." As she looked around at all of them, she noticed Patrick's family off in the distance waiting for them at the school's front door. Almost all of the members of the Rhodes and Flannigan families were there to support Gemma. Claire was overwhelmed with emotion.

They all walked into the school together, bought their tickets, and found a row with enough seats to fit all fourteen of them. The lights dimmed and the curtain opened. Claire could see Gemma in her all-black outfit racing off stage left. The stage lights came up and Claire heard Joss groan. She looked over at her sister-in-law and then Brita said to her, "Mama, Auntie Joss peed her pants." Claire looked over at her sister-in-law once again and saw her grabbing her belly. Realization hit her that Joss's water had broken. Joss made eye contact with Claire. Her eyes were wide with shock. She reached over and placed a hand on Greg's arm who didn't realize what was happening yet.

"Hon, my water broke," Joss said to him, he looked down at her and then the floor. Then he turned to the family with urgency in his voice.

"We have to go," he said standing up.

"I've got the kids, go," Becca, ever the calmest in difficult situations, responded. Joss and Greg walked out of the row excusing themselves as they passed by the rest of the family. Joss held her belly as if to keep the twins from falling out. Greg walked behind her with a hand on the small of her back. Awareness of what was happening dawned on each family member as they passed.

"I'll come too," Margie said as she slowly began to rise from her seat grabbing her purse from the floor.

"No!" they both exclaimed back to her in unison, turning their heads over their shoulders. Claire knew they didn't mean to come off rude. They were reacting to the urgency of the moment.

"Stay here with the family. I'll call you once we are at the hospital and settled," Greg said walking Joss up the center aisle.

She was a bit taken aback but sat back down. The audience's attention had shifted from the action on the stage to the action in the aisles. Joss and Greg walked to the exit. The rest of the family put a smile on their faces at the people around them as if to encourage their attention back to the stage. The show must go on. Shannon and Levi stared at the back of their parents' heads as they exited. Becca quietly moved down the row to sit with them. She saw Joss's seat, cringed a little at the mess, then sat in Greg's chair pulling Levi on one knee and Shannon on the other.

THIRTY-ONE

With all of the excitement of the twin's pending birth, the family decided to cancel their family dinner plans. Margie and George took Shannon and Levi home to wait for news from the hospital. The rest of them were milling around at the front of the school waiting for Gemma so they could congratulate her. Justine brought her flowers. Claire thought jealously to herself, *she never brought me flowers,* but decided to stifle that inner child voice. She was happy her mother did it for her daughter. Patrick leaned over and whispered into her ear, "Why don't you go spend some time with your sisters? I'll take the kids out for a celebratory dinner." Claire looked up at her husband. The man she had been married to for fourteen years and couldn't believe she ever doubted the stability of their marriage.

"Are you sure? I should be there to celebrate with you." She looked at him with uncertainty knowing she would like to do both.

"Go be with your sisters. You've been here for all three shows. Gemma won't mind. Besides, I want the kids all to myself." He leaned down and gently kissed her. Claire stood on her tiptoes and kissed him back. She gave Brita and Grayson hugs, then walked over to her sisters.

"Looks like you are both stuck with me today. Patrick wants to spend time with the kids and suggested the three of us should spend some time together too." Becca glanced over at her brother-in-law. They made eye contact. She smiled at him, he nodded at her. They had come to an unspoken truce over their love for Claire.

"Looks like it's a night for the Flannigan girls." Elana looped her arms into each of her sisters and led them over to Becca's car.

Claire yelled back over her shoulder, "Tell Gemma I love her and I'm so proud of her. I'll call you all in a bit."

***

THE GIRLS PICKED UP TAKE-OUT BURGERS AND FRIES. IT WAS A junk food kind of night, they all agreed. Claire wasn't sure how casual they would be at Becca's house as she had never spent time together there before. When they arrived, Becca took off her shoes and carried the food bags into her living room. She opened the storage ottoman next to the couch and pulled out three blankets, one for each of them. She then walked over to her wine cabinet and took out three stemless glasses and placed them on the coffee table next to the food. "This is my kind of night," Elana said, headed into the kitchen and came back with a bottle of white wine from the fridge. It had never occurred to Claire to help herself to anything in Becca's refrigerator. That was Elana though, she could make herself comfortable anywhere. Her two older sisters curled themselves up on the couch. Elana opened the bag of food and started to pass around its contents.

"Okay, sister confession time. It's been too long since all three of us have been together and that has to change now. From now on we will make time for each other. The three of us." Elana sealed in her proclamation with a large bite of her juicy cheeseburger. Some grease dripped down her hand and she licked it off.

"What do you mean by confession time?" Becca asked as she shoved a handful of fries in her mouth.

"It means we are going to share things we have kept from one another.

No more separate lives, no more secrets. I'll go first." Claire and Becca looked at each other and then back over to Elana. They both assumed they knew everything about their sister as she, at no time, held anything back. "Mark and I are still married. We never officially divorced."

"What?" They both said simultaneously with eyes bulging out. They paused their eating and drinking in mid-air.

"What do you mean you and Mark are still married?" Becca exclaimed.

"Well, we got married because I was pregnant. Yes, we were dating and yes, we were sort of, kind of in young love, but we were not ready to be married. We gave it a go for ten years for Danny's sake. Then when we decided to split up, I knew I couldn't afford to support myself and I needed medical insurance. So, we never got an official divorce. We are still legally married. I've kept his medical benefits, and he helps to support Danny. Oh, and we've been 'friends with benefits' for the last eight years." Becca started choking on the sip of wine she was swallowing, coughing uncontrollably. "It works for us. I actually think I love him more now than I did when we got married. We live our individual lives, and we spend time together. It's the perfect non-marriage, marriage and the sex is great too."

Claire and Becca were speechless. They had no idea what to say. It was clear by her grin; Elana loved the impact her confession had on her sisters. "Wow. You have lived your life exactly as you wanted to." Becca shook her head in disbelief and admiration.

"Why shouldn't I? You have to create the life you want to live," Laney said confidently while twirling her brown hair between her fingers. "Mom and Dad did despite having three kids to raise. They constantly put themselves first. We could have been bleeding to death in the back yard and dad would have told us to wait until intermission to take us to the hospital." Elana laughed curling her feet underneath herself in satisfaction.

"You're right, dad did. Going to work, coming home, eating dinner, watching all his sports on television. But did mom? I don't know if she ever wanted children. I'm sure watching other people's kids and then working in Dad's office was not the life she dreamed for herself." There was so much truth to Becca's statement. All three sisters took a drink of wine. No one had anything to say after that.

"Okay, someone else, go." Laney turned and glanced at Claire. Claire looked at both of them. "Well, you all know everything about me at this point. There are really no secrets left. Becca, your turn." She took a big bite of her cheeseburger, and grease dribbled down her chin, so she quickly grabbed a napkin from the coffee table to catch it.

"Come on, Claire bear. There's got to be something we don't know," Laney said.

"Okay, umm..." she thought for a second, "Brita was named after the water filtration system." They all started laughing. Claire told them the story about Brita's birth, the delivery room, and Heidi, her nurse.

Tears were coming down Laney's face at the ridiculousness and originality of it. "I don't know what's funnier, that you named her that or the fact no one questioned it. Claire, you really need to learn to speak up for yourself." Claire glanced at her knowing she wasn't wrong.

"After I came to my senses, I did look up the meaning of Brita. It is a feminine name of Swedish origin that means 'exalted one,' it's a variation of the Irish name Bridget. It's the perfect name for our vibrant little one," Claire said proudly.

"We love our little water filter." Laney laughed. Claire tossed a throw pillow at her while they all laughed. "Okay, Becca, now it is your turn."

"Well..." Becca said hesitantly and a bit nervously. "I've been thinking about this for a long time." She hesitated and then continued, "I'm forty-four and single. I make a good living. I have my own home. There's one thing missing from my life I really want." Her sisters stared at her waiting. "I want a family."

"Becca, I think that's amazing. Are you dating? Are you on dating apps? Are you going to go solo and get a sperm donor? What are you thinking?" Elana fired off question after question.

"No, not dating or dating apps. No sperm donor." She paused. "I'm going to adopt." Claire and Elana practically jumped out of their seats.

"Holy shit, Becca. That's amazing. Mom's going to hate it." Elana rushed over to her and hugged her, squashing the burger Becca was holding to her chest.

Claire stood up with tears flowing down her face and walked over to join the sister hug. "Becca, you will be an amazing mother. Lord knows you got enough training with the two of us when we were little. I'm so happy for you."

"Thank you both, I'm really excited; I already started all of the paperwork. I'm going to foster-to-adopt. So, there is a lot to do. I have to take classes, have the house inspected and approved, and get people to vouch for my character. It's a lot and...I am excited about all of it. Through my pro bono work, I have met many children in the foster care system being bounced from house to house. I have also met some great foster families and some not-so-great foster families." Becca rambled on grinning ear to ear.

"Wow. Shock and awe are all I can say." Laney moved back to her seat, climbing under her cozy blanket.

"Um...Elana, shock and awe to you too," Claire chimed in. "Do Mom and Dad know you and Mark never divorced?"

"Are you kidding me? Of course not. Mom would be appalled I was staying in my marriage for money and sex. Actually, maybe she would be proud. I'm not quite sure. Anyway, the less they know the better." All three girls started laughing. It was like all of the years of separation dissipated and the Flannigan girls were back together again.

Claire took a small sip of her wine and then stared down into her glass. "Becca, can I ask you a question?" she asked softly. Becca looked at her raising her eyebrows as if to say yes. "Why did you move back home after college."

"Yeah, why did you?" Elana turned her body and attention to their eldest sister.

Becca picked invisible lint off of her blanket. A few silent beats went by before she answered, "Because Mom asked me to."

"And you did?" Elana turned her head side to side looking from

Claire to Becca. Claire could see confusion on Elana's face. She was feeling the same way.

"She had breast cancer," Becca said it so quietly Claire could barely hear her.

"What? Are you kidding me? Why is this the first we are hearing of this? Why didn't she tell us?" Claire felt sick to her stomach. She looked over at Elana who looked as shocked as she was by this revelation.

"Claire, you had just left for college, and Elana, Danny was a newborn. You know how private she is, she didn't want to worry either of you. She's fine; she had the lump removed and went through chemo and radiation. Listen, you guys, Mom was never the mother we may have wanted and she's not going to be. This is something that I've had to learn to accept. I've also had to learn to forgive her so that I could move on. I discovered during that time there are a lot of layers in her past that makes her who she is, but that is a story for another time, for right now, I want you both to know that I made peace with her, and I hope you both can too." Becca finished the last of the wine in her glass.

Claire stayed later than she should have considering she had to work the next morning. Elana decided to sleep at Becca's for the night and head back to the Cape after the morning traffic rush. The three of them reminisced and laughed for hours. They had a little too much wine and Claire had to call an Uber to bring her home. She decided to have Greta take her back to Becca's the next day to get her car. Greta would be so excited to hear all of the events that happened over the weekend. They still hadn't heard from Greg about Joss and the babies. Overall, the weekend turned out completely different than Claire had expected it to on Friday morning.

THIRTY-TWO

Joss was in labor for eighteen hours until they finally did a C-section. It wasn't what she wanted but after that many hours of labor she agreed. They had a boy and a girl, Sean and Lily. They now had two boys and two girls. After the babies were born, Greg leaned over to her and said he loved her, Joss said, "You're getting a vasectomy." This became a classic family story to tell.

Two weeks later was Memorial Day weekend, the family met at the soccer field to cheer Grayson and his teammates on. Afterward, they drove over to Joss and Greg's house to meet the new babies. Elana came up from the Cape with Danny. When the sisters were together, Elana had vowed she was going to do better to be more present in there lives and visit more often. All of the Rhodes and Flannigan families were in one house, together. There was food and baby gifts and kids running around everywhere. Danny, being the oldest, was carrying the younger ones around giving them airplane rides. Gemma was braiding Shannon's hair and Grayson and Levi were in the backyard playing soccer.

Claire looked around. Everything felt right in the world to her. Her mother-in-law walked over to her, "You know, dear. Now that summer is approaching you will obviously have time to take care of the house and kids by yourself, I would think." There was the passive/aggressive tone of hers again.

Claire looked at Margie with a forced smile on her face and replied, "You know, Margie, I don't care if my house is messy and the laundry isn't always done, and there are dishes piled up in the sink. I'd rather spend time with my children, make memories with my family, and have more time with my sisters."

"Well, you know dear, you can have a clean house and time with your family," Margie said crossing her arms at her waist.

"Since you never worked a day in your life I'm sure you can't understand how to balance all of it, but since I am a working mother, I'm choosing my children over chores, but trust me if I need your help, if I want your help, I'll ask for it," she said sarcastically. Her mother-in-law gave her a pat on the arm not registering Claire's tone and walked away.

"Wow, look at you. Standing up to Margie. Looks like our baby sister found her voice." Elana walked over to her carrying a plate of food with Becca right behind her. Claire laughed and stole a piece of cheese off of her sister's plate and popped it into her mouth.

"I think I may have," she said slyly to both of them.

Joss rose from the couch with a baby in her arms. "All right, I love you all but it's time for me to go upstairs. My boobs are bursting, my incision hurts and the three of us need a nap." Joss didn't hold back her words. Greg followed behind her with the other baby.

Elana turned to Becca and Claire. "I want to be Joss when I grow up."

"Me too," agreed Becca.

"Me three." Claire said, and her sisters laughed.

"Here are my girls." They turned and saw their mother walking over to them from the living room. She had on her traditional pair of casual slacks with a sweater and long double looped necklace.

"Hey Mom, how are you? Where's Dad?" Elana gave her mother a hug. Justine looked uncomfortably over Elana's shoulder at her other two girls unsure of what was happening. She cleared her throat after Elana released her.

"Oh, he's already plopped himself down in front of whatever game is on in the other room. Look at the three of you girls together. Your father and I did something right. We raised three amazing women." Justine smiled as she passed through to the dining room to get food, patting Claire on the cheek as she snuck by her. She then turned back to them. "Oh, by the way girls, Dad and I decided we are selling the house. The agent is coming by later this week with a new contract. I'll let you know when we need your help. Okay, time for food for me."

The three of them watched her walk away. Elana shook her head after their mother. "We will finish that conversation about mom's breast cancer battle at some point. Right now, I just want to say," she dramatically paused, put her plate down, and pulled her sisters into a hug. "The greatest gift our parents ever gave us was each other." The sisters all nodded in agreement.

Patrick walked over to them. "Is this a sister's hug only or can I get in on it too?" Becca and Claire unhooked their arms and opened them up to him. As he stepped into the embrace, Claire glanced around the circle. Then she made eye contact with each of them, ending on her husband. "Patrick, looks like I finally won the lottery."

"When the path seems too long and hard, my sisters took my hand and reminded me I don't ever have to walk it alone."

—author unknown

ACKNOWLEDGMENTS

Writing and publishing a book is hard, and I could not have done it without the support of some very special people.

To the first readers of this book, Debra Chute, Mike Haller, Paul Kely, Corinne Smith, and Amy McGuane. Thank you all so much for your encouragement, honesty, and support in helping to bring this book to fruition.

Thanks to my writing coach, Jennifer Graybeal. Your guidance gave me the confidence to author this book. You challenged me, took me out of my comfort zone and showed me that I am more capable than I gave myself credit. You are my guardian angel and fairy godmother all in one.

To my amazing editor, Amy Briggs, your honesty and insight helped bring this book to the next level. You challenged me in all the best ways possible. I am a better writer because of you.

I am grateful to my family for their patience and kindness, and to my husband and children, who always encourage me to keep writing.

My tribe...Amy McGuane, Ali Canada, Lauren Carter, and Charlie Adcock. Thirty plus years of friendship and counting. *We stick together.*

ABOUT THE AUTHOR

Wendy Haller writes across multiple genres. She has published poetry and children's books. She likes to write a bit of tongue in cheek humor with a bite of heart-wrenching reality. When not writing she can be found walking her dog, practicing yoga or snuggled under a blanket on her coach with a cup of tea and a book. She lives in Connecticut with her husband and two children. *The Flannigan Girls* is her debut novel.

Did you enjoy this book? Please post a short review on Amazon, Bookbub, and/or Goodreads. Your reviews help to support indie authors.

Curious as to what Wendy is up to next? Subscribe to her quarterly newsletter at www.wendyhallerauthor.com.

Facebook: wendyhallerauthor
Instagram: @wendy.hals
Tiktok: @wendyhalsauthor

Made in the USA
Middletown, DE
18 June 2024

55601379R00119